For Pops

This is a work of fiction. All the characters, events, places, and organizations portrayed are either products of the author's imagination or are used fictitiously.

STAR PEPPER: A Spicy (Ad)venture in Interstellar Capitalism

A Note about Units:

In this novel, I refer to many units of distance and time that sound familiar. However, they are not exactly the units you, my reader, are familiar with. For example, the current second was defined in 1967 as "9,192,631,770 periods of the radiation corresponding to the transition between the two hyperfine levels of the ground state of the caesium-133 atom." For comparison, the Commonwealth standard second is "10,000,000,000 periods of the radiation corresponding to the transition between the two hyperfine levels of the ground state of the caesium-133 atom." This means that the Commonwealth second is approximately 9% longer than the second you are used to.

Because the Commonwealth runs on math, it strives to make its math easier whenever possible. Many of the Commonwealth species use base 10 number systems, and base 5 is also popular. (This is in itself a strange coincidence. For example, one member species traces its number system back to the number of teats in the dominant mammaloid ruminant raised for sustenance and trade in its early history.) Consequently, a Commonwealth minute is designated to be 50 seconds long, and a Commonwealth hour is designated to be 50 minutes long. This makes the minutes in this novel a little shorter than your minutes, and the hours about 45 of your minutes long. The standard Commonwealth day is 25 hours

long, although planetary days might be different. For example, the day on planet Earth would be about 32 Commonwealth hours long.

Instead of weeks, the Commonwealth calendar is based on tendays, and five tendays are grouped into a pentad. Ten pentads make up a year.

Along similar lines, the meter used in the Commonwealth is defined as 1/300,000,000[th] the distance traveled by light in vacuum in a Commonwealth second. The meter you are used to is defined as 1/299,792,458[th] the distance traveled by light in a second. Because a Commonwealth second is longer, this means that the meter is also about 9% longer than you are used to.

Finally, the Commonwealth defines a standard gravity (g) as 10 Commonwealth meters per Commonwealth second squared. This translates to 9.2 meters per second squared using our units, noticeably less than the 9.8 meters per second squared we feel on Earth.

Most readers should be able to read the novel without reference to these figures. However, some scientifically minded readers might notice the math seems off, which is why this note is included here.

CHAPTER 1

"This time I'm going to save some of my share," Parn said to himself as his heavy boots clanked down the starship's gangplank. He owed that much, at least, to Vigar. The man had gone beyond mentoring the young corer, he had trusted him with his legacy. Parn couldn't let it be for nothing, although that was certainly what he'd done with it so far.

There would be plenty of money to save, as this world was the find of a lifetime. A seemingly endless forest of phase one star pepper trees, stretching all the way to the horizon. And rising out of the canopy of red-brown leaves were the scattered spires of the phase two trees, the real treasure. If it had been found by a wildcatter, he was probably rich beyond imagination now. If it had been pin-

pointed by a corporate nav team, well, they were probably getting an office party this tenday, with free snacks and a cash bar (with a free drink coupon for "Employee of the Pentad"). There might even be comp time for all the overtime they worked to get here first.

"Parnassus, now is your assigned harvest time," the robot said. The voice came to him from the robot's speaker, the speaker in his helmet, and his internal integrated interface (Tri-I). Although the air here was breathable and safe, the helmet would protect him from the toxic gasses given off by the star pepper.

Parn looked over his shoulder at the robot standing behind him. Its ten legs were bent double so it didn't tower over him too much, although this didn't help its appearance, which was already too much like a spider.

"Yeah, let's get going."

"I will take you to our first assigned tree." Spiderbot grabbed him in its four arms, then used its long legs to walk across the canopy, reaching down amid the branches to grab the sturdy trunks of the phase one trees. When they reached the assigned phase two tree, it held Parn out to the trunk. He

stuck his boot spurs into the tree. Then the robot stretched a safety strap around the trunk and fastened it to Parn.

The tree sure looked ripe. The bark was distended outward, so it was likely filling with fluid. Looking down, the network of roots that fed from the phase one trees into the phase two were large and knotty. And the color was a deep brown. Also a good sign. Now it was time for the real test.

Parn lifted the helmet of his suit, removed a glove, and took out a corkscrew-like corer. He screwed it slowly into the bark. He could immediately tell the pepper was ripe. The stench of volatile organic compounds filled his nostrils. When he pulled the core out, he looked at it. It was a dark grey, almost black. Good color. He took the tiniest pinch he could manage and rubbed it between his finger and thumb, spreading it into a very fine layer. Spread out, it looked light gray on his dark skin. As he turned his hand in the light, the fine flecks sparkled. He could feel the cooling effect as VOCs evaporated off his skin. He smelled it: isoprene, acetone, and terpenes. He touched his finger to his tongue.

At this concentration, the burn was intense,

but Parn was used to it, and he could separate out the flavors as he rubbed his tongue along the roof of his mouth. Definitely ripe. A fine flavor, it would probably be graded as zytharine for the mild alcohol and piney hop-like character.

He passed the core over to spiderbot. The spiderbot had three functions. First, to transport Parn, his gear, and the harvested pepper. Second, to taste the star pepper and confirm that it was ready to harvest. Third, to watch Parn to make sure he didn't slip any of the precious pepper into his pockets. Just a pocketful a day would be worth more than his legal share from this voyage. The spiderbot took a small sample of the pepper and confirmed Parn's judgement that this tree was ready for harvest.

Once spiderbot gave the confirming beep, Parn put his helmet back on. He got out his hand saw and began working through the bark. This was all done with hand tools to reduce the risk of explosions. Since that's what the star pepper was for in the first place, exploding to propel the seed pods into space, the risk was great. And if one tree went off, not only could it destroy the entire expedition, it would likely set off the entire grove, a loss that

would make stockholders on a hundred worlds weep.

Once he had cut a hole large enough to enter the tree, Parn pulled the bark off. The putty-like star pepper broke in an irregular plane at the tip of the cone formed by his angled cuts. He handed the bark section to the spiderbot. As the robot held it steady, he started working at it with his curved scoop-like knife, cutting the pepper into chunks about a half kilo each. He handed them to the spiderbot, who wrapped them in tightly sealed plastic, then placed the chunks into its expandable carrier unit.

When he had gotten all the pepper but the centimeter closest to the bark, he began scraping the bark. This B-grade pepper was still valuable, but it was worth much less because its flavor wouldn't be as good, and it was contaminated with bark.

When spiderbot was satisfied that all the star pepper had been removed from the bark section, it discarded it. Then Parn got to work on what was in the tree itself. First, he started clearing the pepper right inside the door. He scooped out half kilo chunks, working downward at first, until he reached the bottom of the chamber. He worked

carefully and quickly as Vigar, a fifth-generation corer, had taught him, probing a centimeter or so past the vertical of his current section to make sure he wasn't too close to the edge, which would affect the quality of the pepper. Although it was hard to identify the chambers from the outside of the tree, Vigar had taught Parn how to see the slight curve of the swollen trunk, so he almost always ended up close to the bottom of one. Once he had removed all the A-grade star pepper he could reach from outside, he started removing the B-grade at the bottom so he could step inside. Then he detached himself from the safety strap and worked from the inside.

Spiderbot stayed mostly outside, but it extended its head and a receiver for the star pepper chunks inside. The head provided light as well as a watchful eye. It wasn't hard work cutting the soft star pepper, but it was tedious and demanding. He had to keep the chunks within 25 grams of the target weight, and he couldn't accidentally penetrate the B-grade layer. Once he had cut into a chamber, he had to clean it all out in one day. The star pepper began drying out immediately when the chamber was opened.

He fell into a rhythm. Like an industrious form of tai chi, he performed the basic motions again and again, working against the resistance of his own muscles—the soft pepper provided none—to create the uniform size, shape, and quality the company demanded. The hours fell away as the pepper accumulated. After he had gotten all that he could reach, he set up an adjustable wheeled platform so he could reach what was at the top of the chamber.

For meals, he hooked himself back up to the safety strap and hung outside the chamber to eat. The air was so contaminated during his first meal break, he had to eat with his helmet on. He attached a tube of food paste to a port and the feeder sucked it through when he engaged the nozzle. On his second break the air was clean enough that he could take his helmet off and eat some nutrient bars. The taste was about the same, but he liked the chewing.

By the time Parn finished, it was well after local dark—the next day. It took more than a full day to clear out a single chamber. There were procedures that could reduce the burden for the individual worker—have two people in the chamber

at a time or have people trade off working in the chamber—but these were either unworkable (two people in a chamber at once was inefficient and crowded most of the time), wasted time (having people wait to get on shift), or risked drying out the star pepper (if people ran late for their shift). So it was one man and one bot per chamber.

After scooping out the last of the B-grade to spiderbot's satisfaction, Parn let the spiderbot grab him and carry him down from the tree. Laden with about 50,000 kilos of star pepper, the spider bot was too heavy to be supported by the phase one trees, so it walked on the ground underneath the canopy, carefully distributing its weight on its enlarged inflatable feet and shining its light on the dark ground. This gave Parn a chance to look at the local fauna.

Star pepper was an invasive species, but it took hundreds of years for the trees to mature, so a harvestable grove had been completely assimilated by local wildlife and some native plant species that could tolerate the toxic soil that the trees generated. Some corers kept notebooks about the wildlife and plants they observed in the star pepper groves. To Parn it was more a casual amusement

that helped keep him awake as he headed back to the ship. If he fell asleep, it would be difficult to wake up and deal with the end-of-shift procedures. It couldn't be more than casual amusement because most of these species would be wiped out when the star pepper exploded.

Back at the ship, the shift supervisors first washed off his suit, carefully collecting the slurry that came off him. This star pepper residue was separated, centrifuged, and sold as C-grade, the only grade that Parn and his fellow corers would be able to afford, and even then it was a luxury that Parn had never been able to fit into his budget. Then there was some paperwork to fill out before he could hit his bunk. Well, not his bunk. With irregular shifts over a day long, it would be inefficient to assign corers to a bunk, so he just flopped down in the first available. He barely had time to dream about how he was going to blow his money before he fell into a deep, dreamless sleep that seemed far too short.

It was when the alarm went off that he focused on saving again. He remembered what it would take. If he could save three-quarters of his share, he would be able to outfit an expedition after just ten

trips. Then he would be able to reach the secret star pepper planet that Vigar had given him the map for. One last coring expedition, and he'd never have to do it again. He'd never have to worry about making rent or paying the power bill or scraping together loose change to afford a nutrient bar. And again he vowed that this would be the time he would start saving his share.

CHAPTER 2

When the harvest was finished, all the robots were disabled and left in a heap near the ship. Their mass could be more profitably replaced with star pepper. Parn knew that if the company weren't afraid the corers might coordinate theft of the remaining pepper, or destroy the ship in a mutiny, they might be left, too.

Instead, the company kept careful track of all personnel and even sponsored a launch party with free food and alcohol. It was a cynical practice, because it allowed them to appear generous without actually giving very much. They knew that the corers would be exhausted from over a tenday of 30+ hour shifts, while the ship's crew—who had been resting during the planetfall—would all be too busy to participate.

But like most of the other corers, Parn made the effort and showed up to the party. Of course, it wasn't like he had a huge number of choices. Two of the cabins had been converted to cargo holds for star pepper. All the corers were now sharing one bunkroom. Although there were hammocks strung in every conceivable way, there were still not enough bunks for everyone to sleep at once.

Some of the greenhorns were sleeping on the floor in the bunkroom or the hall. They would regret that when the blue-and-maroon-clad ship's marines rousted them. Even if they managed to avoid the marines, the extra g's of launch would make them very uncomfortable.

But down in the cafeteria, there were a few of the crash couches available. Parn went by the bar and grabbed a whiskey with a beer chaser. As it was being poured, he looked at the posters on the wall. One of them showed a man peeing on a stage one tree, with his back facing out. There was a red circle and a line through him. The text said, "Don't urinate in the forest. Urine in the suit will be carried back to the ship." The other one had a picture of one of the steins used in the cafeteria. Around the edge a circle of words said, "Yesterday's beer is

today's urine is tomorrow's beer." At the bottom, it said, "Conserve!"

He chuckled because they'd forgotten to change out the posters. Those were planetfall posters and should have been replaced with the launch slate that encouraged him to find appropriate seating during acceleration or take a bracing position. And it wasn't as if they were actual posters. They were virtual posters transmitted to his Tri-I, which overlayed them on the blank wall. They could be changed at the press of a button. But the yahoo whose job it was had forgotten to press the button.

At least the bartender was doing his job. Parn took his shot glass and his stein. Then he found a spot at a table with some of the other oldtimers. He threw back the shot, then started sipping his beer as he tried to listen to Mehany telling her story.

It was a great old one about the days when corers got paid by the gram. She and another corer got in a tussle at the weighing station. It got a little heated until Mehany pushed the other corer, hard, on his shoulders. She was a big woman, and she wasn't kidding around. She pushed him so hard

that the impact ignited the star pepper residue on his suit. It blew Mehany back and blew him clean off the ship. Of course, he broke over 100 bones and died a slow painful death because the ship's doctor couldn't save him, but Mehany told it well, and everyone laughed.

When it was his turn, Parn told one about a defective robot who misread the star pepper residue on his suit as stolen pepper. In the original event, the robot said almost nothing, just carried Parn bodily to the brig. Where he waited for days for someone to check the file and see that everything had been done properly. What he didn't tell about the event was how he got his share docked because he wasn't harvesting for most of the planetfall. That led to some really lean pentads, and once you've spent five tendays being hungry, you can get pretty desperate. He remembered being all but dead from starvation before he was able to get a place on a new ship.

But he didn't tell that part of the story. Instead, he gave the robot some crazy lines that made it the perfect straight man. And when he got to the point where the robot hauled him off, Parn grabbed his

own shirt with his hand and yanked himself out of his chair. Everyone loved that bit.

As he hit the floor, the warning siren went off. They were finally ready to start the return journey. Parn jumped up and got back into his chair. Sensing his weight, the restraints slithered out over him. There was a chorus of clanking sounds as all the steins were held to the tables magnetically and their lids sealed shut. No beer to drink and with his story thoroughly interrupted, Parn just let himself lean back in the chair and wait.

Then the engines ignited and the three g's pressed down on him like a big heavy blanket. Combined with the weight of the tenday of long shifts and short sleep plus the recent alcohol, Parn sank into sleep without even knowing it.

The next thing he knew, he was being roused by one of the ship's marines. The party was long over—his beer was gone—and he had to vacate the cafeteria so those who had been sleeping could now get something to eat. That meant that he, and all the other sleepy corers who were being roused, could now move to bunks to get better rest.

There was a line to get into the bunkroom. Parn leaned up against the wall and looked at the

STAR PEPPER

*A Spicy Adventure in
Interstellar Capitalism*

MATTHEW CANDELARIA

Matthew B. Candelaria

STAR PEPPER

poster on the opposite wall. It showed a picture of a man standing with a phase 2 tree behind him. He had taken the helmet off and his face was turning green. The poster read, "It's not 'Fresh' air: Outgassing from trees can kill." Parn knew a lot of the corers liked to inhale the gasses and get high before they started cutting into the tree.

Vigar had told him that was a good way to get killed, so he'd never done it. And in his own career, he'd seen plenty of evidence to support Vigar's assertion. The toxicity wasn't so bad as the poster made it out, but working hundreds of meters in the air, you needed all your wits about you to keep from making a fatal mistake.

While Parn was waiting, somebody figured out about the posters. The display suddenly switched to show a man with an angry expression standing beside a bed. He was pounding his fist into his other palm. In the bed, a fat man with ugly animalian features dozed. The caption read, "Everyone Is Tired. Give up your bed on time to avoid fights." Parn snickered. They were so late making the change, they had completely skipped the launch slate of posters. This warning was valuable: fights over a bed could get deadly, and because they disturbed all the other sleepy cranky people, they could spiral out of control.

Eventually they'd cleared out enough people, and it was Parn's turn to stumble into the perpetual twilight of the bunkroom—just enough light to let you find your way in and out and facilitate supervision, but not so much that it interfered with most people's sleep. Parn was lucky enough to get a bottom bunk. He kicked his shoes off—shoes in bed was a wakeable offense—and let himself collapse onto the bed. It was still warm and smelled of BO. There was a little drool spot on the pillow. He groaned and flipped the pillow over. The other side didn't smell any better, but it was cool and dry. That was enough. Parn fell asleep almost immediately.

When he was awakened to let the next shift of corers sleep, Parn stumbled out of bed and toward the showers. There was a brief wait, and he said "Hi" to Mehany, who looked as tired as Parn felt. Her dark hair, streaked with gray, was frizzy and untamed right now, and her eyes were barely open between the sagging lids and the puffy dark bags underneath.

They stepped into the white tile antechamber

and threw their clothes into the hamper. The hamper read his ID on the clothes and made sure his alternate outfit was waiting for him after the shower. His one pocket's worth of personal effects—the typical allotment for corers—went into a small plastic container, whisked by robotic hands to the other side of the shower, too.

Naked, they rubbed the chemical cleaner all over themselves. Then they stood under the shower with their eyes closed. They waited. There was a buzz and then the water sprayed down on them for 30 seconds. The cleaning chemicals were highly soluble, and the spray was pretty much adequate to remove it all. What it didn't remove could be toweled off. The towels were black, absorbent, and clean. New underwear, then the blue-and-gray uniform all the corers wore.

He picked up his personal effects. For Parn this was just three things: a comb, a key, and an ID patch that Vigar had given him. It supposedly belonged to Vigar's great, great grandfather. Once dressed and outside the shower rooms, Mehany said, "Ready for breakfast?" She looked much refreshed after the shower. Her eyelids weren't sagging anymore, but the bags under them were still a little puffy. Her chubby face no longer seemed to be weighing her down, and she could manage a smile, though it dispelled quickly.

"Yeah," Parn said. He could probably stay awake through breakfast.

This was the most dangerous part of the trip. It would take them more than a pentad to reach the speed required to jump back through Rho Space to Xythas. Then almost as long to decelerate and dock with trade station Sxthrik. After the anticipation and the work and the exhaustion, the corers had to contend with boredom and cramped conditions. It was likely that some of them wouldn't make it back.

Usually, it was just brawls and fights that killed people. Sometimes a greenhorn thought it might help the math and improve the value of shares if fewer people were splitting the total. They were more right than they knew: being a killer meant you forfeit your share, and it was very hard to get away with anything on the ship where privacy was in such short supply. Despair, suicide, romantic rivalries, disputes over cards, and improvised narcotics all took their toll. Vigar had taught Parn that getting through it successfully meant keeping cool.

Having a few friends was helpful, but no one too close. Mehany understood that, too. So they made a good pair.

At least the crew were all human, so there was one less thing to fight about. This was, like most things, an economic decision. The races in the Commonwealth required nearly 20 different inhaled nutrients, and if you added in the races who participated in the United Market but hadn't ratified the Commonwealth Articles, the number was over 30. So keeping to one species per crew made it easy to satisfy their breathing requirements, not to mention supplying their diet.

And then there was the issue of conflicts. At any given time, there were half a dozen interspecies conflicts taking place among members of the Commonwealth, and the animosity of these tended to be carried onto ships. There were intraspecies conflicts, too, but those were between specific colonies and were less likely to manifest on the ships. The corers were runaways and drifters by nature, and many of them didn't even know the colony where they were born. Those that did were as likely to hate it as love it.

There was a line to get into the cafeteria, of

course, so they stood waiting. The smell coming from the kitchen—something dark green and vegetative was as close as Parn could narrow it down—reminded Mehany of her first husband, so she talked about him a bit. He was a big man, a hard worker, and a joker. But they fought a lot. After a couple visits to the hospital for each of them, they decided it just wasn't working out. He loved his greens, she said.

Parn was not so fond of his greens, and he took the smell of them as a very bad sign. There were usually anywhere from six to ten meals available for the entire trip on a voyage like this, with a couple saved in reserve as surprise additions during the return trip to help boost morale. The presence of greens now meant at least a dozen meals with them before the end of the trip. Not a happy thought for Parn. Still, he was hungry enough to eat them now. He stood up on his toes to see into the pale blue cafeteria. Parn saw that there was a group of corers coming out, probably enough to let them go in.

He was about to pass the happy news onto Mehany when someone hit his shoulder, spinning him around a quarter turn. Parn looked at the man who had hit him. The man was thin and wiry, with wide, intense eyes. He had a knife—not one stolen from harvesting, about the largest knife one could get in as a personal effect.

"Gimme the key, Parn!" the man said.

"What?"

The knife pressed against Parn's uniform, pushing it up against the skin between his ribs. Other people in line saw but barely reacted. They didn't want to get involved. Mehany reacted, though, starting to push forward. Two large men tried to stop her. It was not as easy as they expected. Mehany was built like a rhino and she could go from zero to scary fast in nothing flat with good boots on the gripcoated hallway floor. She knocked into the two thugs, causing them to stagger back. They were too close to hit her, so they grabbed her, trying to wrestle her down.

The man with the knife pushed it a little harder into Parn's side. "I'll split you open and take it."

"You'll give up your share."

"I don't care, that key is worth more to me than a share."

That got people's notice. But it didn't make them want to help Parn. They all started looking at him, kind of hungry like. He didn't like that look at all.

He looked away from the crowd at Mehany tussling with the thugs. One of them looked like he was trying to get something from his pocket, but he wasn't going to make it. Mehany was working him pretty good. "Okay, okay," Parn said. He made as if to reach for his pocket, which focused the attention of the man's intense eyes. Just then, Mehany managed to knock one of the thugs onto their ringleader, and the two of them ended up in a heap. Parn had a nick in his skin and a tear in his uniform.

Two marines showed up in the hall. The men on the ground and their friend looked at the marines. They decided it was time to give up the fight and hurried off. The marines watched impassively.

Mehany yelled, "Hey, ain't you gonna do somethin about that? My friend was almost killed!"

One of the marines looked at Parn with a decidedly unfriendly evaluation. "He looks fine."

Parn felt a chill. "Hey, look, the line's moving. Let's get into the cafeteria." He more than gently urged Mehany away from the marines and into the cafeteria.

Breakfast was indeed leafy greens in a thick broth made with some grain similar to oats. There were also "cheese" biscuits, some "fresh" (probably rehydrated) fruit, and hot tea. The tea was bitter, but it was caffeinated, and it was truly hot, not tepid as it was on some ships.

Mehany remained quiet until they reached a table with a couple of other oldtimers, Craeg and Belial. Then she leaned in and asked, "What was that about?"

Craeg also leaned in and said, "Huh, what?"

Mehany said, "We got jumped by some guys out there, and they were asking Parn for his key."

"What key?" Craeg asked.

"Huh?" Parn shrugged. "I don't know. It's nothing. Probably a case of mistaken identity."

Mehany didn't let it go so easily. "And those marines—they should have caught those guys, but they didn't do anything. What's going on?"

Parn shrugged again, "I don't know. It's gotta be a mistake." No one at the table was convinced, but they knew better than to ask too pointed questions about another corer's past. Although he maintained a calm exterior, inside Parn was screaming, "Oh, shit, shit, shit, shit!" He knew he had run out of time. Even if he could start saving money, there was no way he would save it fast enough to keep ahead of the people who were coming for him now that his secret was out.

CHAPTER 3

Parn survived a couple more confrontations with the knife man before the jump. The man's name was Serl, a corer of fair ability and moderate experience. Parn didn't know him and didn't know how the man'd learned about the key. Did Serl know that the key would unlock the map to a potential pepper planet? Or was he just hired to get it by someone else?

Parn and Mehany were rarely apart, and they started sleeping in the rec room where there were plenty of others that they could more or less trust. Each time Parn was jumped, the marines showed up too late and did nothing. Obviously, a ship's officer knew what Parn was hiding. But they couldn't go after him directly. If it looked like the marines were targeting corers, everyone got nervous about their shares. That had been known to cause a riot, which could quickly spread to all the ships in the convoy. Corers couldn't use their Tri-Is to communicate—these could be blocked—but it was hard to keep them from accessing the ship-to-ship communicators. Entire shipments of star pepper had been lost that way.

Almost as bad would be validating the rumor that what Parn had was even more valuable than shares. That would create a different kind of riot. Every man for himself, at first, then warring factions, and the marines wouldn't be able to keep order. And the shipment could be lost again. Because there was no privacy on the ship, every confrontation was in public, and people started talking. With little else to do but speculate, people were starting to come up with wild theories. And then the confrontations stopped. Parn thought he would be safe until the ship docked—if he were vigilant.

Once the ship jumped through Rho Space everyone began talking about another worry: pirates. Realistically, trying to hijack a star pepper convoy is idiocy. Any weapons you might use to try to disable and board a freighter were likely to set off the cargo. And then you've equipped an expensive piracy expedition with nothing to show for it. So mostly space pirates were a product of corer folklore.

Of all the elements of corer myth, nothing was more feared than the floaters. These were pirates of some unpopular alien race that had a low metabolism, something resembling reptiles or insects or mollusks in some vague way. These pirates set up a huge nanofiber net, millions of kilometers across the popular shipping lanes. When a ship got caught in the net, they used some mechanical means to climb along the net to reach the ship, assembling on the hull. The pirates would then cut into the command center of the ship, kill the crew, and evacuate the atmosphere of the corers' quarters.

Never mind that the physics were ludicrous. Even if there was a net strong enough, catching a ship at the speeds it would be moving after a jump would kill the floaters with the sudden jerk. Not to mention the speed they'd have to travel along the net to reach the ship before it pulled into port. Never mind that a ship's decelerating engines would melt through pretty much any net rather than letting the ship get caught. Never mind that no such thing had ever been reported in any reputable news outlet on tens of thousands of worlds over the thousands of years that star pepper had been harvested. Those are facts, and it isn't facts that drive the talk among corers, it's rumor and superstition.

The companies were happy to take advantage of these rumors and superstitions. They switched the posters again, warning people to be alert to signs of danger. They gave minor rewards like free beer or a meal upgrade to people who brought in validated tips. They even allowed corers to go out on supervised sweeps of the hull to check for floaters. Cheap diversions. Anything to keep people occupied until the cargo could be brought profitably home.

Parn was happy to take advantage of these rumors, too. After a little while, the story of his key had been told and retold so much that it had been dissociated from his name. It had been embellished with all kinds of details and would fit nicely alongside the stories about superintelligent aliens they had encountered on the planet. You know, the ones that were indescribably beautiful and craved the kind of bestial pleasures they could only get from lower life forms. Space mermaids. Star angels. Pepper gods. They had different names, but it was always the same story. The evidence always lost in the final pepper explosions, so the stories had a mythic half-truth to them. Disbelief of them was also a defense. If you believed the stories were true, then you had to acknowledge that gods, angels, mermaids, and corers—especially corers—were ready sacrifices to the pepper trade.

Like most corers, Parn knew that the stories about floaters were completely impossible. But like most corers, he couldn't dismiss them. At first, just a few vehement supporters told the stories. Whether they were true believers or just trouble-makers, Parn couldn't be sure. But over time these stories got repeated and they seemed more possible. Then probable. Then factual.

Parn even found himself on a floater sweep. In the airlock, the marine in charge reminded them of the procedure. "This is a simple survey. All we're doing is spreading out along the meridian until you can just see the person next to you on either side. Then you look up and you look down. If you see something, report it when we get back inside.

Do not try to engage a floater if you see one. Do not leave the meridian."

It sounded simple enough, but when it was Parn's turn to step outside, he realized why this was a stupid thing to do. Inside, the deceleration simulated a nice, comfortable gravity that kept you anchored to the floor. Outside, though, it turned the hull into a sheer cliff, completely smooth except for the one safety ledge that ran along the halfway point of the ship, the meridian. And all around the cliff was the void: blackest space dotted with bright lights. Most of those bright lights were stars billions or trillions of kilometers away. A very few of them were planets, merely millions of kilometers away. More of them were ships, which might be mere thousands of kilometers away. None of them would be any help if you fell out into the void.

But most likely you wouldn't fall out into the void, you would fall "down" toward the base of the cliff. And at the base of the cliff the brilliant blue fire of the engines would consume you in an instant, scattering your atoms across the entire system.

Lost in thoughts like these, Parn didn't notice at first that the people on either side of him weren't spreading out properly. Instead of spacing out so they could see around the entire circumference of the ship, they were keeping close to him. Parn clicked his com and said, "Hey, greenies, we're supposed to be spreading apart."

Instead, one man got closer. Close enough that Parn could see into his helmet. Serl.

Parn tried to back away, then bumped into the man on the other side. One of Serl's lackeys. He was trapped. He looked up the side of the hull, then down toward the blazing engines. The lackey grabbed Parn's arms. They swayed unsteadily on the narrow ledge.

"Watch out, fool," Serl said. "If you tip him off, it won't do any of us no good."

Parn and the lackey pressed up against the hull until they were steady.

Serl said, "They told me to back off, that it was done. But they didn't think about this opportunity here. But I saw it. This fool expedition is perfect. I'll just split you outta that suit and get the key."

"Who told you to back off?"

"You don't need to ask me that. Wherever there's pepper, there's money. And that's what this whole ship is about, ain't it? Pepper money. And you've got a secret stash."

"You've been had," Parn said. "This isn't your first expedition, so don't be a chump. Think about how many times you've heard the rumors about a secret pepper planet. It's like pirates or mermaids. Just stories people tell to pass the time on ship or add spice to their tales of the voyage. You'll be giving up your share for nothing."

Serl hesitated. Then he shook his head. "I don't care. They tells me to get the key and they'll pay. It's their problem if there ain't no planet."

Serl raised his hand. He had a short length of pipe or something in it. A club. He raised his arm and then brought it down as hard as he could onto Parn's faceplate.

Parn flinched. He wasn't too scared. He was pretty sure the stories of people accidentally breaking their faceplates open were phony. And with the tiny ledge they were standing on, Serl couldn't possibly get enough leverage to break open the faceplate. Could he? Still, the sound of the club on the faceplate was unnerving. It reverberated through his helmet and rang in his ears.

The challenge for Parn would be getting past

Serl and back into the ship without falling off the ledge. The lackey was holding his arms, so he had that much less ability to hold on to the ship. But the lackey was also not holding on with his arms.

Parn spun his torso, fast and hard. The lackey was startled and his first instinct was to grab more tightly onto Parn. That was a mistake. The torque pulled his feet off the tiny ledge. He began to fall. Parn would fall, too, but he raised his arms suddenly, freeing them from the lackey's grip. As he fell, the lackey grabbed onto the side of the ship with magnetic boots and gloves. It slowed his descent to a gradual slide.

Serl was startled, frozen with his club raised high. His expression of grim determination turned to shock, then fear. Parn took a moment to steady himself against the side of the ship.

Parn could practically see the calculations going on in Serl's mind. There was no way he was going to get the key now. With his friend dead, it might only take Parn's account of events to cost Serl his share. Parn had to die, too. He let go of the club and readied to push Parn.

Parn crouched under the push. Then he thrust his helmet forward, hitting Serl in the pelvis. He used the tiny ledge for all the support it was worth, trying to hold on with his toes, but having to depend on the way the boots were shaped to fit with the meridian. It was enough. Serl was dislodged from the ledge with a grunt. He began to fall, then just barely managed to cling to the hull a short way down, above the head of his lackey, who was trying to climb up, but was losing ground badly.

Parn did a different calculation. They didn't have to die. And maybe if he saved them, they could tell him who else knew about the key and maybe the map. "Listen," he said. "Don't try to climb. It will just make you slide faster. Hold tight, and I'll try to get the rescue line."

Parn edged along until he caught sight of another suited figure along the meridian. He clicked his com, "We need the safety line. Two men have fallen."

The company maintained that, for humans, bringing out the safety line was not only unnecessary, it was potentially dangerous. Under normal circumstances, the magnetic boots and gloves were enough to keep people on the meridian. The safety line caused an additional distraction that could cause people to get tangled or dislodged. Parn knew this had been appealed to the United Market Labor Safety Board (UMLSB), but upheld. Right now, the insanity of not having a safety line out all the time seemed clear to Parn as he waited for the message to get relayed to the airlock, and the line to be relayed back out.

When Parn got the line, he headed back along the hull to where they had been on the far side of the ship. He looked down, and though Serl and his lackey were far down the hull, almost lost against the brilliant blue exhaust of the engine, Parn could see that they hadn't listened to his advice. Both the men were frantically trying to climb along the hull and they were steadily losing ground.

Although it made him feel unsteady, he contorted his body to make sure his antenna was pointed at the two shadows below. "Stop climbing!" he yelled into the com. "I've got a line, so just hold tight!" They didn't respond. They probably didn't hear him because of the extreme interference that close to the engines.

Parn slipped the rescue line through a local anchor point and began to feed it out to the two men now far below. Momentum took it as fast as he let it out, but not fast enough. The lackey slipped over the lower edge of the ship and tumbled into the blue light. He evaporated.

The line wasn't quite within reach for Serl. Parn called down, "Hold tight, and I'll swing it to you."

Serl saw the line and tried to scramble for it. He lost his grip on the wall and in a second he was gone, too.

After the sweep team was back inside there was a brief inquiry. The crew didn't care, but they had to check off certain boxes on the UMLSB Incident Report. Parn could have probably said anything he wanted, but he chose his words carefully. "There were space pirates. We fought them off. Serl and the other man fell." He also recommended that they should reconsider the use of safety lines for floater sweeps in the future. He did not know whether that was included in the report or not.

Word that there had actually been space pirates on the hull went through the ship rapidly. People talked about it daily. They frequently asked Parn for details. He generally just said he didn't want to talk about it. "Traumatized," people concluded. Sometimes, Parn overheard stories about how he and Serl had long been friends. Other times, they were secretly lovers. A lover's quarrel became the reason why Serl had jumped Parn with a knife. Everyone seemed to have forgotten about the key. Parn knew, though, that someone had set Serl on him. An officer setting corers against one another. He also knew that someone hadn't forgotten. They were just waiting for the right time.

When the ship's main engines shut off, the excitement level among the corers became a tense, caged fury. Everyone was required to assemble in certain areas, waiting for their disembarkation time. Parn and Mehany were class "C" for cafeteria, so floated weightless by the walls as they waited. By random determination, class "C" would be disembarking after class "R" (recreation room), but before class "B" (Bunk room). No food was being served.

"You take your pill?"

Parn nodded. For the last tenday, they had received notice about what they had to do to acclimate themselves to the air, food, and water of their destination planet, Xythas. Basically, for humans that meant taking pills to neutralize the high levels of arsenic in the environment. It turned your shit and urine pink or even red, which was alarming at first, but had no other side effects.

Mehany said, "They'll try to take you aside between the pay station and the shuttle. Once they've been paid, everyone gets a lot calmer. Complacent. Compliant. There's almost no risk of a riot."

"But we're also not under their control anymore," Parn said. "The transfer station is Sxthrik Port Authority property. They can muscle me around, but they can't order me."

"But it's hard to say which is worse. Because they don't have a choice, they might get a little rougher."

Parn nodded again. "Maybe it won't matter, though. If I can get a Port agent involved. Then the company will have to produce documentation if they want to take me."

Mehany shrugged. "Could go either way. Some agents, they see a corer have a dispute with the company rep, even a marine, they're gonna say that's probable cause and sign off on taking you into custody. Then you're in trouble, cause then it's official. Then you need to prove why they should let you go."

"Naw," Parn shrugged. "I don't think so. I think it'll work."

"If you say so, but I'm not going to be by your side when you try this little stunt. I don't need to get run in again."

They fell into silence as they waited for their turn. Then class "C" was announced. Pulling themselves along the handholds, they filed out past the marines who were making sure they made an orderly exit through the chemical sniffers. Just in case someone had figured out a way to get into the hold and thought they could get some star pepper off the ship. Also supervising the exit was the flight crew. The captain looked tired but happy. He was waving at everyone and exchanging pleasantries whenever the line stopped, as if it were a pleasure cruise. The first mate looked bored, detached, and tired. The second mate, Astreyan, had a tight, forced smile. Until he saw Parn. Then his smile disappeared.

Good, Parn thought. At least I know who I'm facing now. He felt better about his chances, too. Since he was the only one who noticed Parn, it was probably a personal gambit. That made sense. The company might give him a pittance of a commission if he turned Parn over, but if he obtained the information on his own, he could become insanely rich. Being personal made it easier for Parn. Astreyan might have influence and he might have money, but he couldn't leverage his official status against Parn, not without raising questions.

Now Parn wondered: how did Astreyan find out?

At the chemical sniffers, Parn held his wrist up to the reader, which accessed his Tri-I and confirmed his identity in the 20 different ways required by the United Market Covenant on Payee Verification. This authorized him to claim his advance on his share, which would be disbursed at the next station.

When Parn passed the pay station, he made a beeline for the shuttle. The transfer station lights were different, close to the natural light from the primary—Parn thought locals called it Bolas, but he and other immigrants called it Xythas—as seen from the surface. It technically overlapped with the human visual range, but it wasn't a lot of overlap. Especially in these artificial lights. If it weren't for the regulations requiring reflective strips that could be seen by all visual species, Parn probably would've tripped over the chairs in the waiting area.

Beyond the chairs were several Xythan officials waiting. Parn couldn't remember whether they were natives here or long-ago settlers. They had four limbs, each ending in a three-toed foot. These they used for handling large, heavy objects or for attacking if you made them mad. They packed a wallop. Their bodies were kind of lumpy and misshapen and in this light they mostly looked grey.

Before he could reach the shuttle, three Human marines cut him off. "Come with us, sir," said the leader.

Parn said, "What? Why? I'm just trying to make my shuttle. Please, let me go."

"I'm sorry, but I'm to take you into custody."

"What? No—huh—there must be some mistake."

"No, no mistake." Now the men were starting to put their hands on him.

"Help," Parn called out. When the nearest official didn't respond right away, Parn made it sound more urgent, "Help!"

That got attention, and the official walked over. When it got close, it reared up onto its hind legs, bringing its sensory stalk up almost to eye level with the humans.

"What's going on?" the Xythan asked. It spoke the Market Tongue with flat precision, never deviating from the 95% perceptible range. The sounds came from an airtube at its shoulder, the breathing orifice that could be utilized for speech. Parn knew that when talking amongst themselves, the Xythans used both air tubes simultaneously, which made it very difficult to speak or understand Xythan, even if you were fluent.

Parn spoke quickly to get his words out before the leader could speak up. "These men are trying to stop me illegally!"

The Xythan pivoted its sensory stalk to look at the lead marine. "Is this true?"

"We've been asked to hold this man for questioning. He's suspected of trying to steal star pepper." The marine didn't do a good job of staying in the 95P. He was getting emotional, and the trembling of the Xythan's sensory stalk meant it wasn't hearing the marine very well.

The official looked at Parn, then back at the marine. "Do you have a warrant?"

"Our ship just pulled in. We haven't had time."

The official writhed the tendrils around its mouth. That was a gesture that Parn knew well: irritation. "You could have beamed your concerns forward and had them evaluated before."

The marine pulled out several sheets of paper. "This man has a history of stealing star pepper."

"Hey!" Parn said, "that was an administrative error. The charge was never proven, and I was released as soon as it was reviewed."

The official writhed its mouth tentacles even more vehemently. "That's why you send all the documents ahead so they can be evaluated by a true judge. I don't have time to review these now. Release the man until you can find a quality warrant." The lead marine's face got hard for a moment, then he decided not to keep up the fight. He let Parn go.

Parn said thanks to the Xythan official. He didn't say anything to the marine—he didn't want to make things worse with him. His name tag said Mejit and the set of his eyes told Parn that he had made a personal enemy of the marine. Time to get to the shuttle and hopefully get quickly out of sight.

On the shuttle, Mehany had saved him a seat.

The big open shuttle was almost full, with maybe just a couple extra seats. Next to Mehany wasn't necessarily the best place to be—she was a little larger than the seats allowed for so she tended to crowd into the next seat, but her friendly smile made Parn happy.

"I wasn't sure that was going to work," she said to Parn.

"I wasn't, either. But Xythans like their rules, so I thought there was a good chance."

The shuttle bumped away from the transfer station, then gave a little jerk out of orbit. It roared through re-entry, then coasted to a landing. With no bags, the shuttle unloaded quickly. Although it was midday, the human port area was illuminated with powerful spotlights to make up for the thick air that let little light penetrate in the human visual zone. On the ground, Parn found that things always became a little awkward. Before Parn could say goodbye, Mehany grabbed him by the arm and pulled him close.

"Don't forget me, Parn. When you strike it big with whatever it is you're hiding, you give me a cut."

Parn put his hand on Mehany's shoulder and

pulled her even closer. Their cheeks touched. "I guarantee that if I can find you, I'll make sure you get your share."

And with that, the two separated.

The problem was, Parn had no idea how he was going to capitalize on his secret: the location of an undiscovered star pepper planet. But now he had to work quickly. Anonymity had given him a lot of time to be working toward a solution. He should have been saving up his money to outfit an expedition, but he had failed at that.

To be fair to Parn, the shuttle port was not set up to allow corers to save their money. It was full of all kinds of gaudy attractions that a corer, flush with money and primed by confinement and boredom, found hard to resist. His Tri-I was programmed to filter out many of the ads, but it didn't get them all, and the Tri-I company also sold ads in his visual field. In the span of just a few blocks, a corer could find himself deprived of all his hard-earned share, with no option but to turn back toward the center of the port to ship out again. Parn had done that many times, but he couldn't let himself do that now. Not only did he need the money, he couldn't stay anywhere he was known.

As he walked, Parn saw two inexperienced corers from the ship studying the board outside a brothel. This not only explained the prices, but the grid was color-coded to show how compatible the species were. Purple spaces meant that intercourse between the species in that particular gender combination was safe, unlikely to cause injury to either party. Yellow indicated species combinations that could potentially cause injury to one party, though this wasn't necessarily a hindrance to pleasure. Parn knew some people who liked to be with species that had claspers that could be used to choke them. But species combinations that were coded blue were dangerous and definitely not recommended. For humans, that included anything with bony or chitinous genitals that could cut off a fleshy appendage or were designed to pierce the flesh.

The men were talking, but they were nervous about going in. Although he didn't dare stop, Parn wanted to share his wisdom—it was best to try many things. You needed options for when your port of call didn't have whores of your species.

Of course, Xythas wasn't one of those. After the Xythans, humans made up the largest component of the population. When the Pepperzazz Corporation set up its branch office here for star pepper exploration and exploitation, it brought tens of thousands of humans to staff its offices. Since the office opened, the human population had grown, and now there were millions of humans on Xythas.

Thinking of the brothel reminded Parn where he might go outside the port. He might visit Chatter. Chatter worked as a nav calculator for the Pepperzazz Corporation. He had come down to the port to get a little excitement. Parn remembered when he met Chatter. The man had hired a whore in the yellow category, but, apparently, it was a little more dangerous than he'd bargained for. He was trying to argue for a refund on the basis that the species should be coded blue.

Parn saw the situation and knew it was about to get ugly. He helped Chatter understand he wasn't going to get a refund and that persisting just made him likely to get a beating. Then he gave Chatter a few suggestions about what to try next.

Chatter was so happy with the suggestions that he sought Parn out later and bought him a couple drinks. He even offered Parn the option of staying with him sometimes. Parn took advantage of it every once in a while, but not so often that it was likely anyone knew about the connection.

Before he could visit Chatter, Parn had to retrieve the memory crystal with the planet's coordinates on it. He didn't think he was being followed, but he wanted to be sure. He ducked through stores and the streets crowded with corers recently arrived from his caravan. He slipped into a brothel he didn't normally frequent and came out wearing different clothes. The john had been a bit upset at the intrusion, but he quickly calmed and happily parted with his clothes thanks to some cash compensation.

After that, Parn took a circuitous route, but didn't actively make evasive maneuvers. He didn't want to look at all suspicious on the security cameras in public areas. He knew the man looking for him didn't have authorized access to the cameras, but he wanted to make sure that it would be as hard (and expensive) as possible to track him down by bribing the individual owners.

Parn eventually found himself at the bank of public lockers where he had stashed the memory crystal. He used the key to open the locker. Then he took out a pair of glasses that would help him see in the dominant spectrum. Many humans had their eyes augmented to let them see well in different spectra, but that had never been in Parn's budget. Finally, he grabbed the crystal along with the small amount of cash that was his savings from all the previous expeditions. It was pathetic, barely a twentieth of the pay from any one expedition. But that didn't matter now. He didn't have the time to save anymore. He had to find an investor and equip an expedition, quickly. Unfortunately, he didn't have any idea how to do that. He hoped Chatter would.

CHAPTER 5

As he rode the train, Parn held the memory crystal in his pocket. He didn't release it once during his journey. Vigar had given it to him. It was supposed to go to Vigar's son, the way that Vigar had received it from his mother. But that plan got ruined when his son died in a brawl over a card game on a return trip. That broke Vigar up pretty badly whenever he talked about it.

Parn got off the train and climbed onto a magnetic lift to the street. After a quick wisp of travel up from the subway, he stepped off the disc and onto the ground. Behind him, the disc rose, then turned to descend as other people climbed on to get back down to the transit level. Few vehicles drove in neighborhoods like this, where the streets were covered with the short, sturdy blue-green native grass. At least, it looked blue-green through the light-shifting glasses. Without the glasses, everything looked grey.

People walked freely on the grass or on the paved paths in front of the shops. Mostly humans in this neighborhood, but a few Xythans. Above the shops were residences, including the one where Chatter lived. The entire neighborhood was made of pre-molded buildings. There were perhaps a dozen different designs, and looking up and down the street, he saw several repeats of each. The concrete paths had a pale-yellow cast to it that was typical of Xythas, but also made a pleasant contrast against the grass and faintly blue-green sky.

It took Parn a few moments to remember exactly how to get to Chatter's place. It had been a few trips since he had visited the nav man. Then he remembered. The entrance to the residences was between two restaurants, one of which had gaudy orange windows, the other had more modest yellow ones. Both were lit in Human-friendly spectra. Parn stepped into the small lobby and signaled up to Chatter. He didn't answer, and Parn realized he was probably at work. Parn vaguely remembered something about that from the last time he had stayed with Chatter, but not enough to know when to expect his return.

So he went to the restaurant with the more plain windows and sat down to wait. He ordered a beer and a local delicacy of fried tubers he had grown fond of since moving to Xythas.

As he ate, Parn thought about Vigar. He wondered why the old corer, after losing his own son, had adopted Parn. It wasn't like a dad could get to know his son really well as a corer. One or both of them were always shipping out. And they couldn't ship out together. When a child received their certification, they were allowed to ship out with their parent once during their initial five trips. After that, they got put in the random pool like everybody else, and only allowed to ship out with any other crew member once every five years. The companies wanted to reduce the risk of conspiratorial crews assembling, but it meant that Vigar had only seen his son once in the last ten years. That didn't matter. Vigar had loved his son deeply and was in a bad decline since his death, until he met Parn.

Ironically, it was the same rule that brought them together. Parn's first voyage as a corer was from his home port, but because of the rule it would be at least three years before he could ship out again with a new Human crew. So he had to go somewhere with a larger Human population. Xythas was the first good candidate available. And it was on his first trip from Xythas that Parn met Vigar.

Parn immediately recognized the wisdom of Vigar's easygoing ways. The stillness that let the world rush around him, acting only as necessary. This reserved attitude conserved his energy and made him ready to seize any opportunity. And Vigar had returned Parn's admiration by giving him the greatest opportunity possible in the form of the map to an undiscovered pepper planet. And so far, Parn had done nothing with it. Now that he was being forced to act, he felt he had neither the energy nor the readiness to deal with it.

Parn had finished his food and ordered a second beer before he saw Chatter. He chugged the rest of his beer and rushed out to intercept the navigator.

Chatter was tall and skinny. His skin was pale. His eyes were pale. His hair pale and curly. He wore a blue one-piece uniform that befitted his position as navigator, albeit with several personal patches. From previous experience, Parn guessed that these were likely related to recorded entertainments he followed. He couldn't be sure, but he thought that all of them had changed out since the two men had met last. Despite the change, none of the patches matched any stories that Parn himself followed.

Parn came up aggressively, buoyed and oblivious because of alcohol. Chatter was taken aback and may not have recognized Parn at first.

"Chatter, it's me, Parn. You mind if I stay with you a couple days? I just got paid so I can pitch in for food this time." He put out a hand.

"Yeah, sure," Chatter said, and grabbed Parn's wrist. Parn grabbed his wrist and the men shook hands. Parn noted absently that their Tri-Is were updating contact information. "For a little bit. Any idea how long?"

Parn wasn't expecting that question. Chatter didn't normally ask. "I dunno. Just a little while. I'm in a bit of a spot. Maybe if you help me, it'll get me moving along sooner."

Chatter scratched the back of his neck. "I know corers think that we at corporate have some kind of influence. We don't. At least, not most of us. And if I did have influence, I don't think it would have anything to do with that."

"To do with what? You don't even know what I'm asking. It has nothing to do with corer assignments if that's what you're thinking." Parn put a hand on Chatter's chest. "Here, I jumped in too fast. Lemme get dinner. Which restaurant do you like better?" Parn pointed at the restaurants on either side of the residence entrance.

Chatter indicated the one with the orange windows. "I like the Kierday special."

"Great, I'll grab some beers, too."

"Wine, please."

"Wine, right." Parn remembered that here, wine meant bonberry wine. "Go upstairs, settle in, and I'll come up with dinner."

Chatter's apartment smelled like a mix of cooking and trash. Stale spices and rotting vegetation blended in the air. When Parn went to the kitchen to open the food and drink, he saw why. The disintegrator unit was broken, so waste was being held in a bag in the kitchen. The bag was full to overflowing and its translucency revealed that fluid was accumulating in the bottom.

The food preparator was full of residue, dried on and crusted. Chatter noticed Parn's hesitation. "Prepper's broken," he said.

"Your place used to be real nice," Parn said. "What happened?"

"I . . . I've been hard on it." Chatter's hesitation had a strange quality to it, like he had a lot more he wanted to say. Instead, he just looked down, away from Parn's eyes.

Parn knew there was a warning there, and if he had any other option, he would be out the door in an instant. But he didn't know any other navigators. And he needed a navigator to check the crystal so he could start looking for investors. Vigar had taught him that much. Parn opened the drinks first. A wine for Chatter, beer for himself. He handed Chatter his drink, then said, "Cheers." They touched bottles. Parn took a quick swig.

As he went back to the kitchen, Parn ran the odds that Astreyan had learned of his connection with Chatter. It seemed virtually impossible. At least, not that fast. He knew he couldn't stick around, but there seemed no way Astreyan could've tracked down such an obscure link so quickly. So, whatever was bugging Chatter, it wasn't that he'd been contacted by Astreyan.

Parn brought back the food and asked Chatter what was new. Chatter said nothing, then went on for half an hour about his work, the apartment, his work, his commute, his work, the local market, and his work, constantly (and unnecessarily) reminding Parn how boring it all was.

By the time Chatter paused in his running commentary, giving Parn an opening, both men were finishing their second bottles. Parn figured it was time to pitch his scheme.

Chatter got a weird smile on his face. "I knew it was something like that. I dunno whether Murien will be more proud of me for refusing this temptation, or more angry at me for letting you in in the first place."

"What?" Parn said.

"Look, I got into a lot of trouble since I last saw you, and I might say it's your fault, but Murien wants me to acknowledge I had the power all along, and it's my fault I fell to temptation.

"So I'm going to remind myself that I have the power to resist your temptation. I can choose not to succumb to this. Not like whoring. Not like gambling. I lost all my money that way. But this? This I could lose my job over. And that's the last thing I've got. I won't let you take that away from me, too."

"Woah," Parn said, "wait, stop. So that's what happened, you spent your money on gambling and whores?"

"Well, not the whores so much. Gambling, though. Gambling just takes and takes and takes."

"I know that. But surely you don't blame me for that?"

"You introduced me to them."

Parn laughed. "You weren't gambling with the corers, were you?" Chatter nodded. "Those guys will bet everything they have because they know they can just get on the next ship. They don't care. Because they can't get credit, they don't get in debt. But you, you probably have great credit and can get in a lot of debt."

"Had great credit. Now I have no credit. Just a lot of debt. Murien says it's good for me. I'm on a strict budget, and Murien says budget equals control."

Parn had been thinking that Murien was a girl-friend, but all of a sudden he looked around and realized there wasn't a single feminine touch in sight. Nor were there any images of a woman who might be a girlfriend. So who was Murien?

Then Parn noticed a message pop up on a

portable device sitting on Chatter's table. It had a string of slangy ideograms that he thought looked feminine.

"Is that Murien?" he asked.

"No," Chatter said. "That's just Ana from work." He held the unit up so Parn could see the screen. It seemed to be an invitation for Chatter to come to a ballistic spacecraft launch. "She's always wanting me to go to these things. She loves them, but Murien says that corporate could consider that kind of hobby to be side work—like your little project—and it could cost me my job."

"So, who's Murien?"

"My counselor. She helped me get straight after all the mess you caused. No, not you. She says it's not your fault."

"You told her about me?"

"Yeah."

"By name?"

"Yeah. There's no harm, right? It's not like anyone is looking for you."

Parn felt a cold sweat form on his palms. That's how Astreyan could find him, quickly. Parn had to get out before Astreyan and his cronies arrived.

Parn rushed out the door. In the hallway, he

heard the elevator opening. And over it, the voice of the marine who had accosted him at the transfer station. "I hope he's here. I want to catch him without the Port Authority around."

Parn backed into the apartment, then realized he was trapped. Chatter said, "What's wrong?"

Parn looked at him and said, "People *are* looking for me. They're coming to your door. Stall them." Parn had no illusions that Chatter would be able to put them off for long. He needed to think of something quickly. He opened a window just as the door announced visitors.

"Hello?" Chatter said into the apartment com system.

Looking out, Parn saw that there was a mould line on the building just below Chatter's window. It was about half the width of the ship's meridian, and it was tapered—not designed to be stepped on at all.

"Chatter Coleridge?" Astreyan asked through the com.

"Yes, that's me. Who are you?"

"We have a report that you've been fraternizing vertically."

Parn decided he didn't have many options. He

stepped out onto the mould line. The narrow part flexed under his weight, but he could just barely manage to support himself on the line by standing on his toes.

Chatter said. "Ha-ha. Me? Ha. Ha. Yeah. Come in."

Parn was outside before the door opened. He scooted along the mould line. He didn't know how long he could manage to stand on his toes like this. He heard several pairs of boots enter the room.

Astreyan said, "So, you were visited by this corer, Parnassus Jackson?"

"Parn? Yes."

The boots were moving around the room. Astreyan's voice came from a different part of the room. "Where is he?"

"Ha. Uh, he left."

"When did he leave?" Astreyan's voice was louder now. Firm but not angry.

Parn clung to the side of the building. His calves were starting to get tired. He needed a way to get down, and though there wasn't a cluster of fusion engines below him, it was still too far to jump. Perhaps if he could lower himself down, but he wasn't sure he'd be able to hold on to the mould line.

Parn didn't hear Chatter's response to the question. The next thing he heard was Astreyan asking, "You don't know? Give us some idea. Was it recently?"

Parn didn't know how much time he had. He thought about jumping, but it looked too far. Then he saw it, a bit of sprue sticking out along the mould line. That he could hold on to. He leaned over and grabbed it.

Just as he was putting his second hand on it, a voice behind him said, "Hey, boss, he's out here!" Startled, Parn lost his balance and didn't get his second hand on the sprue. He dangled by one hand and looked up as Astreyan leaned out. "Suck in a sump," he muttered.

"Should I shoot him?" the first voice, a burly ship's marine by his uniform.

Astreyan shook his head. "I don't want him dead. We don't know where the memory crystal is. Keep an eye on him. We'll try to get downstairs."

Parn knew his situation wasn't going to get any better hanging around here. He let go of the sprue and fell to the ground. They taught corers how to fall without getting injured. Parn had always thought it was silly—nothing would help if you were falling from the side of a stage two star pepper tree. But here, a little tuck and roll worked great. As he got up and ran, he heard a gunshot, and a round hit near him. At first he wondered if Astreyan had changed his mind, then he heard cursing behind him and realized the marine had unwisely fired on his own initiative. Since he hadn't been hit, Parn took this as a good sign. Any time they spent arguing was time they weren't coming after him.

Parn didn't wait for the next disc down to the trains, he jumped into the hole. Fortunately, the spacing between discs was such that he didn't fall too far, though he almost rolled off the side of the disc. He was standing by the time the disc reached the subway level, and he stepped off. A quick cash payment meant he was through the turnstyle and on a train before he saw Astreyan or a marine in the station. Panting as the train pulled away from the station and through the airlock into the vacuum tube, Parn wondered where he could possibly go now.

CHAPTER 6

Not knowing where to go, Parn kept riding the train. He had been a bum before, but he'd never been hunted. He didn't know what to do next. He didn't feel he could go back to the port district. Everyone there would know him, and doubtless many people would be looking for him. In the port, Astreyan's money would buy him a lot of eyes—and hands, too, when the time came to seize Parn.

Parn had only one plan, and it wasn't a good one. In fact, it was a terrible plan, and he knew it, but he didn't think he'd come up with a better one.

On the trains, Parn felt a measure of safety. Astreyan hadn't gotten the law or even the Pepperzazz Corporation involved. Astreyan had influence, but Parn thought he couldn't look at the transit cameras or fare logs to track his movement, the way law enforcement might. That was the difference between being hunted by an individual and being a criminal on the run. But for Parn the consequence was the same: he couldn't go back to where he'd been. All the people he knew, he couldn't see. All the places he knew, he couldn't be. And the life he knew, he had to leave behind. If he returned, it would have to be as someone else. Parn could not be a corer anymore—he had to become a shiprunner.

Part of him was so terrified at the thought of trying to become a shiprunner that he just wanted to give Astreyan the crystal so he could simply sign on as a corer.

But he was disgusted at himself for even thinking that. He had an obligation to Vigar: the crystal had been in his family for generations. At any point, they could have sold it for a small fortune. But the fact that they hadn't said that they wanted to keep the planet and its bounty in the family. Perhaps it was a romantic gesture, a call back to the days before the great corporations had taken over the star pepper trade, but they had wanted the family name on the planet.

When Parn had accepted the crystal, he had assumed the mantle of family, and he felt he had to honor those wishes. Parn knew that if the planet had trees, they would likely be mature. Maybe. The way the story was told in Vigar's family made it sound that way. Vigar's description of what he was giving Parn made it an expectation that Parn should outfit an expedition and harvest his legacy.

It was all just stories until he had a navigator who could look at the data and see what it really meant. That brought him back to his present challenge: how to find a navigator. Chatter was the only navigator Parn knew. And now he knew no-one who would help him. He did, though, have one clue where to find one: the message from Chatter's fellow navigator regarding the ballistic spacecraft launch.

Murtoz, the city where the amateur spacecraft launch was supposed to take place, was far to the south, but the train was fast. Parn had plenty of time to get there and ask around for the location of the public rocket port. Since the city was near the equator, it was a popular place for launches, and there were actually three public rocket ports. Parn checked them out, and he found the one he thought was most likely. All he had to do now was wait to execute his terrible plan.

Murtoz was a picturesque city. It had tall blue-green hills on one side, and a deep purple bay on the other. With its pleasant climate year-round, it also attracted artists of all kinds. They drew and painted its picturesque waterfront—long since given over to rich yacht owners and their assorted parasites. Writers populated its winding streets and rolling hills with their tragically doomed lovers. They videoed dramatic confrontations and chases in its blind alleys.

So tourists flocked in the artists' wake. It was the most popular tourist destination on the entire world. And this combination also made it popular with bums and beggars. Bums and beggars are always the most colorful members of society, and when you bring together the bums of a hundred species in a place so photogenic and appealing, it is a sight not to be missed. Aggressive policing had removed the bums that were crazy and dangerous, so all that were left were the merely amusing, or too aware to let on that they're dangerous. And these lived in a largely peaceful coexistence with the tourists and artists, while they were gently nudged away from the areas the yacht owners frequented.

There was a funicular up the side of the hill to the public launch site he wanted. It was privately owned, so Parn didn't trust it to not share information. Instead, he climbed up the side of the hill. The steeper parts of the path were made of stone steps carved out of the bedrock. The shallower slopes were grass paths. It was a tough climb, and periodically Parn stopped to catch his breath and look back over the city.

Historic Murtoz clustered close to the water, but new districts sprawled out across the valley, even ascending the surrounding hills. As he got higher, he could clearly tell which other hills also had launch sites.

Over the water, sea fliers coasted in the steady breeze. There were several species, but all had thin, membranous wings stretched between their limbs and their bodies. Looking at their grace in the air, it was hard to believe they were related to the Xythans. But, then again, maybe they weren't. Parn still didn't remember if the Xythans were native to the planet.

At the top of the hill, there was a barrier warning about the possibility of rocket blast. Next to the gate, permits hung, showing who had reserved the site for launches, and a schedule showing their times. Parn thought Chatter's friends were supposed to launch around mid-day. The schedule showed a launch about that time, and it looked like people were bustling around in preparation. Parn took a breath and opened the gate.

The rocket, a pre-fab plastic model, was already on the platform. The conning tower held it upright. The payload cone was vibrantly painted with an inexpert design that showed the name of the club.

Parn walked out into the blasted area. A Xythan moved to intercept him, asking who he was. Parn spoke loud enough that he hoped everyone in the club heard him, saying he was a friend of Chatter's.

As he'd hoped, one of the rocketeers said, "Chatter? Is he coming?" The slender human came over to him and he could see that under the gray duster most of the club wore, it was a woman. She was a little shorter than Parn, and looked younger, too. Her face was freckled, her short hair brown with red highlights, and her eyes hazel.

She had a big smile, her face marked with grimy streaks, and she had red circles around her eyes showing she'd been wearing the goggles that now rested on top of her head. "Is Chatter coming? I'd hoped to get him out again."

"No, I don't think so. He's concerned that this could affect his job."

The woman shrugged. "Yeah, that's what they say, but, I dunno. It seems like I oughta be able to use my time to do what I want, even if it's more navigating." She looked Parn up and down. "You don't look like a navigator."

"No, no. I'm a friend of Chatter's. I'm a corer."

"Corer? Well, that's another thing that could cost Chatter his job. Vertical fraternization. Definitely discouraged."

"That worry you?"

"Me?" She shrugged again. "No. My time, my choice. But it worried Chatter." Her eyes lit up. "Say, are you Parnassus?"

"Yeah," Parn admitted, and instinctively glanced around at the other members of the club. No one seemed to be paying attention. They were all involved in pre-launch preparations.

"Chatter talked about you."

"So I'd gathered. Anything that worries you?"

"No. A while back, when Chatter seemed to be a good guy, he talked about you in kind of a boastful way. He was proud of taking that kind of risk, I think. Being with you gave his life some color. It was good for him. And then you left." There was an accusation in her eyes and in her voice.

Parn put up his hands. "I'm sorry, it's just part of my job. It's how I earn my living—not everybody gets steady checks."

The woman sighed. "Yeah, yeah, I know. You weren't Chatter's babysitter, anyway. He should've been able to take care of himself. Only he wasn't. And he got hurt. Bad. I think coming out to the launches would help him feel better."

Parn said, "I agree. I encouraged him to come. I even wanted to give him an opportunity to be something more than a slave to his job." As he started speaking, he wasn't sure what he was going to say, but by the end he'd decided to take the risk of a vague allusion. He wanted to see how she reacted.

"Yeah?" she said. Her eyes sparkled. She offered her hand. "My name's Ana Denk. You say you're not a navigator, but do you know anything about rockets?"

Parn shook his head.

"Then just stay out of the way while we finish our preparations. Over there, in that shelter you can watch the launch if you want."

Parn looked at the rocket. It seemed cheap and fragile, and he fully expected it to explode on the launch pad. Still, he didn't think that would be a bad spectacle. "Sure, I'll stay."

Despite the flimsy appearance of the rocket, the launch went off without a hitch. Although the collector vents took in much of the exhaust to be converted to energy for the city, the flames still licked against the defensive shielding as the club members sat and cheered in the bleachers. The bleachers were only about half full with the club members, their friends, and family who came to watch the launch. Speaking with some of the other members, Parn gathered that for many of them, this trip was an annual occasion that they combined with a family vacation. The spouses socialized. Kids played their own games, some of them right through the launch.

Although many of the club members had people who came to the launch, Ana didn't. Parn could kind of tell why. Although they were ostensibly watching the launch together, she was so engrossed in her portable display/control unit that he was practically alone. He didn't understand the telemetry she was looking at, and her periodic commentary washed over him in waves. Feeling dumb as a rock, he could only say, "Yeah?", "Really?", and other equally uninsightful remarks. He understood, though, that the vehicle was inserted into the right orbit and was operating under its own thrust before Ana turned to him.

"So, what about this opportunity you offered Chatter?" she said. "Can I have a crack at it?"

Parn was startled. The rapidity with which she went from almost completely ignoring him to suddenly thrusting her full attention on him took him aback. He became defensive. "I dunno. I don't wanna talk about it here."

"No? Then let's get something to eat. I'm starving!"

Ana led Parn out a different path. Not through the public entrance, but through another door in the blast shielding, then winding through the sound absorbers, which hummed as they slowly shed their pent-up vibrations. Parn was just starting to panic at the sense of being lost when Ana opened the door to an outdoor courtyard with statues and benches, surrounded by food vendors working out of vehicles and trailers.

Ana took Parn to one of the carts and ordered food for them both, though she let him choose his drink. He recognized one of the beers on offer, so he picked that. She told him he was going to love the food as they took their plates of steaming, dark-colored noodles to an isolated bench. She devoured the noodles with singular focus. Parn picked at them. They tasted okay, and he was hungry, but he was nervous.

He had always known this was a terrible plan. Now it was turning out poorly and he felt trapped. Ana's enthusiasm was even scarier than Chatter's reticence and betrayal. Part of him wanted to run away, but part of him knew that, bad as it was, this was his only plan. His only hope. Fleeing now would only lead to failure.

When she finished eating, Ana checked the progress of their vehicle on her Tri-I. She used an external display to explain to Parn what was happening. She also checked in with a few members of the club for technical conversations. When one of them was almost drowned out by the sounds of Xythan children playing in the background, she switched from the handheld unit to her internal visual and audio relays. Parn assumed it was because it was easier for her to isolate the sound and not because she was trying to hide what she was saying.

After a while, she went to another vendor for a second plate of food—fried meat of some sort. The duster billowed out behind her like a cape as she moved quickly across the courtyard. Parn worked hard to finish his first plate about the same time she finished her second. When she went for a third, she offered to pick him up something more. He acquiesced.

Parn was amazed at how much she ate for how small she was. But, he thought, she probably didn't eat much when preparing for a launch. And she was young. And she probably used up a lot of energy. She was so intense. As she ate, she didn't say anything to Parn. Her eyes kept settling on him with an intense curiosity, but she restrained all the questions he knew were there. Despite the intensity of her gaze, the silences weren't awkward. Much less awkward than when she was talking tech at him and he didn't know what to say. In the silence, they were just two people sitting and eating together. Parn figured out she was giving him time to think of what he wanted to say, and what he didn't. He became relieved and began to relax and enjoy her company.

After finishing her third plate, she looked at her portable unit again. Then she said, "There's another launch supposed to happen here soon. Let's grab some beers and watch!"

They bought four beers from one of the vendors and went to an open area on one side of the hill. It was covered with low plants that had small leaves like clover, but with stronger, spongier stalks. It was immensely comfortable to lie on. There was another member of the club there, but he and Ana just exchanged a cursory nod. Parn could see that one of the launch sites had a rocket on it. It was larger than the one Ana's club had launched earlier, and it cast a long shadow down to the city below in the sinking sunlight. The pink sky was turning a deep purple, and on the far horizon, a few stars were starting to come out. A chill was falling, and Parn was glad their beers hadn't been served cold.

During the launch, Ana talked to (or maybe at) Parn. She must've had magnifying optics, because she commented on people moving around at the site, minutely describing the technical details. She also talked about the beer, how comfortable the ground cover was (not a native plant, imported for the purpose several generations before when Xythas became a major port in the Star Pepper trade), and the stars (apparently, two of them were planets, and one was the trade station Sxthrik where the pepper Parn harvested was being unloaded, portioned, and graded).

After the respite of silence, Parn didn't find this onslaught of words to be troubling. Instead, it was part of the comfortable surroundings enfolding him. No doubt the beer helped, and the spongy leaves supporting his body, but with every detail she shared about what she saw, he felt he was seeing it more like her. The foreign world she inhabited was slowly becoming his world, too. She put an arm around him, and he found that her slender body was as warm as it was dynamic. Conversation abruptly stopped when Ana noticed the people had cleared the launch site. He could feel her anticipation, and it became his anticipation, too. He really wanted to see the launch. And when the rocket ascended on its magenta plume of flame, he wasn't surprised that he was cheering as loudly as she was.

After the launch, they walked down the hill with a moderate crowd of people leaving the park. Some had been watching the launch, but others had just been enjoying the park until it grew too dark to play their various games with balls, disks, nets, and other projectiles. From below, music and light was calling them.

As they got close to street level, the music was loud, the lights bright, and the crowd thick. Ana couldn't hide her disgust. "The entire town is like this now. Let's get off the street—my place is this way!" She led him down a curving street that was crowded, loud, and smelly to a narrow doorway. The stairs up were quiet, and even in her room they could barely hear the din filling the street below. The light was another matter, though, until she closed the shades, and then they were suddenly in almost complete dark, sliced through by light slipping around the edges.

Most of Parn's recent sexual experience was with prostitutes. That always involved a lot of negotiation. And his other sexual experiences, they involved negotiation, too, just of a different kind, so he wasn't prepared when Ana advanced on him suddenly. She kissed him abruptly and was undaunted by the fact that he wasn't prepared to kiss her back. She pushed him onto the bed he barely knew was there. She let her heavy duster fall to the floor, and then she climbed on top of him. She quickly had the clasps on his clothes undone. She knew what she was doing and could do it easily in the dark. It didn't take long before they both were trembling, spent, and sweaty on the bed. Parn wanted to say something, but he wasn't sure what. Ana didn't seem to need him to say anything, so he just let her hold him until he fell asleep.

Parn woke up to Ana's screams. The noise from outside had died out, but the light still sliced around the shades. There was also the pale bluish light coming from a console in front of Ana. "Do you know what you have here?"

"What? Huh? What are you talking about?" Naked, wet, and sticky, Parn was standing on the bed, trying to balance despite his disorientation.

"You have the coordinates of a star pepper planet!" She was pointing at the screen with one hand. The other held a sweet roll. She had pulled on some clothes, a flimsy robe that hung half-open over her freckled frame.

"What?"

"Look, look! Those seeds you have the coordinates and velocity for, they probably (99% possibility) entered this unsurveyed system, here! And there's a 90% chance that there's one or more suitable planets in that system, and an 85% chance that those seeds landed on one or more of those planets."

"Wait, you mean that these coordinates probably do lead to a star pepper planet?"

"Yes! And do you know what happens when you find a star pepper planet?"

"You get filthy rich."

"Of course, but not only that—you get the right to determine shipping lanes in the system. Do you know how many lanes, how amazingly intricate the calculations have to be for that kind of traffic?"

"No, no, I don't," replied Parn, pulling a coverlet over himself. Her question brought him back to the moment, and suddenly he realized. "Hey, you went through my stuff while I was sleeping."

Ana was not to be deterred, "Yes, but, look! Just

look! It's a completely unsurveyed star system. The value is tremendous!"

"Yeah, but you went through my things while I was sleeping. You have no right to do that."

"No, no, you're right," Ana said, folding herself up onto the chair, all except the one hand that was pointing at the screen. "But this is what you wanted, right? You can't get funding for an expedition or even sell the coordinates without a navigator signing off on it, so you needed me to look at it. You just couldn't ask. So I needed to get you out of the way." She gave a childlike smile and took a bite of her roll.

Parn felt he might be in trouble of losing control, so he said, "How much do I owe you for certifying the data?"

"Forget that! I'm your goddam partner!"

Parn wasn't sure he objected.

CHAPTER 7

Ana knew the process of applying for funding. In fact, she knew it inside and out. She had been an adjunct to the wildcatter funding division, so although her course calculations were only a small part of the process, she had studied the entire thing from beginning to end. In training exercises, she'd even played a wildcatter seeking funding, and she dove into the role with gusto.

First, she checked her calculations a few times. Depending on the permutations she applied, the odds that the seeds had landed on a suitable planet ranged from 80-90%, always well within the investment zone. The quantity of seeds gave a nearly 100% chance that if the seeds landed, enough would have sprouted to create a sustainable population. It was over 1000 years since the data had been taken. This meant that the trees had had several hundred years to mature, putting them in the optimal maturity zone. By all measures, this was a claim that any banker would jump on.

So the next step was to get a certification crystal. The certification crystal was a complex data storage device that allowed the bank's computers to verify the calculations of projected course and landing information without revealing any of the identifying information to the bank. These were nearly impossible to hack, and had never been forged, so the crystal would speak to the legitimacy of the claim.

Also included on the crystal was the provenance of the original data crystal that Parn had inherited. Without looking at the data itself, an expert confirmed where and when it had been purchased, and where and when the data had been written and accessed. All of this data confirmed what Vigar had told Parn, right down to the lifeboat where his ancestor sighted the seeds while awaiting rescue.

Once the crystal had been properly encoded, it was time to start talking to bankers. Ana arranged meetings with three different banks on three different days, allowing them to cancel later meetings if the first proved fruitful. The financial centers were technically in the same megalopolis as the space-port, but each commanded its own "town," where it controlled everything. There was corporate branded housing, where employees got amazing deals on rentals and "purchase." Although one could technically own a dwelling in these districts, much of the rights of ownership remained with the corporation. People couldn't change the exterior appearance of their dwellings, and the corporation reserved the right to approve any sales.

There was even branded public transport that they had to transfer to once they reached the border. As non-employees, they had to have a confirmed appointment to enter the community. The first bank was run by Xythans, so much of the branding was lost on the humans, as it depended on having visual receptors in the ultraviolet range. But they couldn't mistake the aesthetic of squat buildings. All the buildings looked as if they were made of wet sand poured in a pile. Even the head-quarters of the star pepper financing division, although it was very tall and relatively narrow, still managed a squat appearance.

From the moment they entered the suburb,

Parn felt uneasy. This wasn't the first corporate town he'd been in. It wasn't that the light skewed more to the UV than was completely comfortable. It wasn't that the doorways were too wide at the bottom but uncomfortably narrow at the top. It wasn't that all the writing was in Xythan. Parn had been on this world long enough that he was completely comfortable with Xythans. He had spent plenty of time in spaces designed for the convenience and comfort of Xythans, with accommodations for humans and other races added as an afterthought—or not at all if they were below the threshold set by the Alien Races Accommodations Act. He was completely unphased by alerts to his Tri-I like: "Feeling dizzy, human? Remember: Xythan exhalations include carbon monoxide." In trying to pin it down, Parn put it on the advertisements.

There was something about the writing and the images that bothered him. He could read Xythan quite well. He was familiar with Xythan images. The populations were so mixed that everywhere he went, Parn had seen advertisements and notices for Xythans, sometimes more, sometimes less. But these made him feel alien in a way that wasn't related to something so concrete as his species. The images, the poses, the phrases, the slang, all seemed obscurely foreign.

Looking at Ana, Parn noticed she didn't feel the same way.

Parn's feelings increased significantly when they entered the bank proper. Inside, the lobby had the same liquid aesthetic. Even with the spectral shifting glasses, the colors were dull. Most of the counters, desks, and workstations were squat and textured to accommodate Xythan preferences.

Ana guided them deftly to the right area for their appointment, but Parn felt the immediate attention he gained when he entered. No one stared. No one even seemed to notice, except for one guard who was visibly watching Parn. But Parn could feel the attention he was getting, from the corners of eyes, and all the electronic ones that could focus on him without betraying their attention.

After a moment's waiting, a human loan officer took Ana and Parn to an office. They put the certification crystal into the console to verify that all the calculations were as promised. It was clear they were working with a junior loan officer, whose only real function was to interact with human clients. They had no power to decide. The time they took looking over the documents was purely pro forma. After a time, they said, "I'm sorry, but we can't invest in this opportunity."

"Why not?" Ana said.

"Well, Ms. Denk, there are many variables we have to take into account in a situation like this. We want to make sure our investment is protected against all manner of pitfalls, and it seems that this one has too many risk factors."

Ana made some quick gestures on the console surface between them, calling up some of the abstracted calculations. "But didn't you see the probability for a true find? A large grove of potentially mature stage II star pepper trees? This is as close to a sure thing as you'll find!"

"We don't believe so," the officer said, and they subtly glanced at Parn.

Parn didn't know why Ana was bothering to argue with this officer. Nothing could come of it, so far as Parn could see.

"Are the orbital calculations off? I checked them several times."

"No."

Ana said, "I want to talk to your manager. I don't think you've really looked at this."

To Parn's surprise, the officer summoned their supervisor. The Xythan came in quickly, as if they had been waiting to be called. A look of recognition flicked between Ana and the Xythan.

She said, "I've worked on a lot of claims that end up being financed by this bank. None of them are as good as this one. The trajectory, the number of seeds, the system they're entering—everything works out as pretty as can be. So I don't see what's the problem. Why can't you finance this expedition?"

"The problem," the Xythan said quickly, "is you. We don't believe you are capable of heading this expedition." The Xythan conspicuously didn't look at Parn the entire time they were in the office, though they were clearly aware of his presence.

Their next two appointments were similar. At the end of the tenday, it seemed to Parn they were infinitely further away from getting funding. He felt an abyss had opened under him, and he was hanging over it, clinging as hard as he could to

Ana's shoes, while she kept checking and rechecking the math.

Then one night, Ana rose from bed after making love and announced the solution. "All we have to do is make it so you're not a corer anymore." She was looking out the window, and not at him. The pink light from the window revealed a quarter silhouette: high cheekbones and sharp chin, but not her nose. Throat, shoulder, the curve of her slight breast through the window of an akimbo arm. Hipbone, muscular leg flexed so that her weight partially rested on toes of her slender left foot. The rest of her was in darkness, melted into the shadows of the room.

Parn sat up. The sheet fell from his shoulders and pooled in his lap. "I'm already not a corer anymore. I can't go back, you know."

"I know." She turned, briefly becoming more illuminated, and Parn could see the largest freckles on her shoulders and chest, but as her back was fully to the window she became completely shadowed. Just a black shape outlined in pale pink. "But, still, you are. The way you walk in the bank. The way you talk. And, most importantly, the way you dress. Anyone looking at you can see that you're a corer. We have to change that."

"We can't change that."

"Yes, we can. The key is the clothes. We'll get you new clothes."

"And what about my walk?"

"I can teach you how to walk. All you have to do is inhabit the clothes."

"And what about the way I talk?"

"If you look right, I can do the talking. You'll be my client. I'm the navigator. I've got the numbers. And the numbers will seal the deal if there's nothing to throw it off."

"And being a corer throws it off?"

"Well, yeah. You're not a professional."

Parn couldn't see her face. "I get paid, don't I?"

"Everybody gets paid for something . . . you get paid for shitting."

"Coring isn't shitting!" Parn threw the sheet off him. The moving air was cool on his damp groin. He started to get up out of the bed.

"No, wait. That's not what I meant." Her tone changed. Parn still couldn't see her face, but he could see the way her head tilted, her back arced and her arms reached out to him. She wasn't the sharp shadow anymore: her body had become as curved and soft as her bony frame allowed, and the words didn't come from hard darkness. "I meant, you have to think like a banker. To a banker, a corer is an alien. More alien than any species. You live in the docks. You work on another planet. You don't have credit, right?"

That struck Parn. He understood that mattered, but it had always been a point of pride that he had never needed credit, never even asked for it. "Yeah, so?"

She got back on the bed, on her knees. Now the light illuminated half her face. Her eye was wide, and the moisture reflected the light. "Well, you understand what credit is, right?"

"Credit is possible debt."

"Yes, but credit is also trust. It's how much a banker trusts you. No credit, no trust. Asking a banker to invest in a man with no credit would be like asking them to invest in an expedition into a black hole! We have to convince bankers to trust you." She moved across the bed on her knees until she was just out of his reach.

"But buying clothes won't get me credit."

"No, it doesn't have to. As my client, your

credit is privileged information. All your clothes have to do is not give them a reason to believe you have no credit. Then I vouch for you with my credit, and they're satisfied."

"But why do you trust me?" He stepped back toward the bed. He was looking down on her now, and he could reach her arms, but he didn't.

"Honestly, I don't." She laughed. "I trust the numbers." She put her hands behind her head and let herself fall back on the bed. The light fell across her body, with her breast, her small belly, and her pubis casting long shadows across the left side, her face turned just enough to be fully illumined. "And I trust myself to manage all the technical stuff."

Parn climbed back onto the bed. He was on his knees at her feet. "So what do I do? How can I help?"

She turned her face just enough that half was in shadow again. "You can get new clothes. Get out of the way of your own success."

"I can do that, I guess." Parn let himself fall onto his back beside Ana. His weight bounced her small body into the air. She laughed and turned toward him as she landed, falling partly on him.

"And when we get to that grove full of pepper

trees, you can claim them and core the hell out of them." Her breath on him was hot, moist, and vaguely ketonic. Just enough that in combination with her words it reminded him of the scent of raw star pepper.

"Yeah." He kissed her and held her. His eyes were closed and his brain full of images of coring: hanging outside the tree with the ground so far below, cutting his way into the trunk, carving out the chunks of pepper, looking out from the dark interior at the gleaming robot watching him from outside in the sun. He smiled, and his soul filled with love. But if asked what he loved, he could not have said.

CHAPTER 8

The club was Ana's idea, too. She wanted Parn to get some practice just hanging out in the clothes in public so he would feel comfortable in them. Parn wore one of the nicer suits he was supposed to wear to the bank. Ana wore a midnight blue dress that sparkled in the light. He was not sure that this club was the right choice. It was too popular, too high profile. It was so famous that even Parn had heard of it. And its reputation scared him.

The club was themed after the initial period of trading with the Zzazzazz, the oldest starfaring race still extant. The Zzazzazz were reclusive and didn't want to trade with the other peoples of the galaxy. But their advanced technology, incredible wealth, and interstellar maps meant they were the most desirable trading partner possible. Everyone frantically sought something to trade with, and that's how star pepper got started. The ZZazzazz loved the stuff and were prepared to pay a high price for it, although they were still very restrictive about the contacts between their people and the outsiders, allowing trading posts only at the very edge of their star systems.

So the club was called "Heliopause." It was far north, isolated from any city. It had a transit pod hangar, not a train station. Emerging from the hangar, you were taken up an elevator to the entry hall. This mimicked a space port. The tunnel from the hangar to the club was partially open, with the frozen tundra outside serving as an effective stand in for the surface of a cometoid where the trading post would be located. The landscape had even been carved to create a false horizon, making you feel you were on a tiny body in space. The only thing they didn't do to make it more realistic was negate gravity.

The club itself had four rooms. One of them was the trading area proper. It was decked out with long tables like the ZZazzazz liked to trade at. The second room was themed like an amateur ZZazzazz museum, full of artifacts. Many of these were truly valuable and rare. Sometimes scholars came to study them. They studied in small cages against one wall. The third room was supposed to be a lab where researchers were trying to understand the nature of the technologies they had been shown. It was full of lights and sparks. But it was the fourth room where Ana wanted to take Parn. It was the Corer Room, and it was decorated as if it were the inside of a stage II star pepper tree.

It was a little large for the inside of a tree, but not much bigger than the largest tree Parn had personally cored. He could believe they got that big. Along one curved wall, it had stairs carved into the side to allow travel up to the second floor of the room, where the bar was. The room was also designed with skew proportions that made it look just a little off. The floor slanted, as did the tables. It made Parn feel a little dizzy right away. A plaque helpfully explained that sometimes when working in the trees, corers became drunk, even delusional. He knew that was a problem in the old days, but if you followed procedures, it didn't happen to you. This was a carnival trick, a way to make a corer's life flashier for public consumption.

Ana led them right up to the bar and ordered

a salt gin for each of them. Parn knew it was the right drink for the period, but he could never get over the seaweed taste. So he ordered himself a chaser—a light beer with just enough flavor to wash out the seaweed. He almost reached for his money, then remembered he wasn't carrying any. Nor would they take it. It was all on Ana's credit.

As he drank, Parn was fastidious in following Ana's directions. He stood the right way, walked the right way, and, above all, focused on her and his drinks, never once looking around to see if other people were looking at him. After a while, she said, "See—no-one's looking at you. They all accept you. You're one of them."

For the second round of drinks, Parn went to the bar and ordered on his own. He could feel it. No one was noticing him. It was a welcome change after the time he spent in Chatter's neighborhood, or, especially, the bank lobbies. When he got back to the table, he dismissed it, "It's a bar. Everyone's drunk. They're not thinking about it."

"Maybe. But this isn't just a bar. This is an elite club. People come here to see and be seen. Seeming not to notice is part of the con, but, believe me: they're noticing." Ana looked around casually, seeming not to notice. Then she leaned in close and said, "Yeah, you're accepted. And if you can pass here, you can do it in a bank. You walk and let me talk." She settled back in her chair, a satisfied smile on her face.

As Parn was finishing his second drink and contemplating a third, a ruckus rose from the lower room. There were some hoots, some laughs, and some applause. He looked at Ana and saw that she didn't know what was going on, either.

Then it was clear what had happened, because coming up the stairs was Saicy Maris, part owner of the Heliopause. The reason why Parn knew about the Heliopause, in fact, was because she was part owner of it. She wasn't a major star in recorded entertainments, but she was in the ones that Parn liked. They were simple, trashy, and in them Saicy took her clothes off, a lot. Parn had probably seen 90% of her skin many times over. But that didn't diminish his desire to see the other 10%, not one bit.

Saicy was voluptuous, and she was dressed to show herself off. She wore a multicolored dress that skewed slightly magenta in the balance. It pulled tightly on her figure, with her deeply tanned breasts almost squeezing right out of the low-cut top. Her light brown hair fell over her shoulders and cleavage in loose curls. She wore very high heels that picked up on the dominant color in her dress. They pushed her ass up, creating a potent, sinuous profile. Parn could not believe his eyes, and he could not tear them away. A bodyguard and a slender robot assistant climbed the stairs behind her.

Saicy raised her hand and called out a greeting. After the loud response, she said, "Are we all having fun?" to which there was an equally uproarious response. Parn couldn't find his voice, but he clapped enthusiastically. Saicy walked up to a white-haired older couple at the closest table. They seemed out of place, being largely indifferent to the ruckus. As she approached, it became clear that the man was deliberately avoiding looking in her direction. "Look at you two," she said to the man and his wife, "how adorable you are." She leaned over the table, her breasts bulging even more forward in the shift. The man's eyes faltered, glancing quickly at the cleavage, but fixed themselves again in the middle distance. "What brings you two here tonight?"

The man didn't seem to trust his voice. The woman answered, "It's Cid's birthday. Just grabbing a drink after a show."

"Wonderful! Stay for two. Or three! The third one's on me." She nodded to the robot, who acknowledged with a slight electronic chirp. "You are so cute," she said to the man and leaned in closer, planting a kiss on his cheek. She left a large, red impression in her lipstick. It only took a moment for the lipstick to vanish in his deepening blush. "I love you," she said as she stood up, gesturing with her hand the way you might wave goodbye to a puppy.

"We love you, Saicy!" came a yell from the back of the room. A table of loud and rowdy men.

She smiled, shook her hips, and blew them a kiss. "And I love you, too!" But she didn't head toward them. Instead, she headed toward the bar. She seemed a bit unstable in the high heels, which surprised Parn. She often wore heels that tall, but with grace. She got a cocktail and drank it at the bar, her backside toward the room. As she drank, she joked with her bodyguard and periodically made comments to the robot. When she told a joke, she twisted her right foot, which shifted her ass noticeably, and when she laughed, every cell seemed to tremble with joy.

Parn pulled his eyes away. Mostly. He couldn't help turning his head just a little and watching out of the corner of his eyes. Ana tried to engage him in conversation. Twice. Then she said, "Oh, yeah, you belong here, all right!" She stood up from her seat and left her half-finished drink at the table.

"No, wait," Parn said, but he suddenly became very self-conscious. He didn't dare get up and chase Ana as she stomped down the stairs, blue dress sparkling angrily with each heavy footstep. Parn swallowed. He decided he would finish his drink and then go looking for her.

As he was just about to finish, Saicy came walking by his table. Suddenly, she started to tilt and fall. She would have hit the ground, but Parn leapt from his seat and caught her as she was halfway down, easing her into the chair Ana had just left. Her flesh was soft as her heavy, curvaceous figure settled into his hands. Her breath was warm as she let out a "whoo." Her soft brown eyes looked a little unfocused, their pupils wider than Parn would expect for the moderate light in the room.

"Are you okay?" Parn asked as her weight settled into the chair.

"She's fine," Saicy's bodyguard said.

Saicy leaned heavily on the table. "Keb, back off."

When Parn was sure she was stable, he slowly released her, staying close in case she should lose her balance. Parn spared a glance for the bodyguard, who, in Parn's opinion, had been too far from his charge. The square-jawed man was impassive, his eyes intense. Parn took a half step back, but readied to respond.

"Keb, I said back off. Gimme some space. I'm fine, now." Then Saicy looked at Parn. Hair was falling in front of her face. She swept it to the left, allowing her eyes to catch the light. She seemed better. "It's this room," she explained. "The proportions always throw me off. When the designer came to us with the idea, it seemed like fun. He called it a carnivalesque plan. But I swear I lose it in this room at least one night out of ten." She sighed, then gestured at the drink in front of her. "Is your friend coming back, or can I finish this?"

"I can get you a fresh one," Parn said, almost standing up.

"No, no, no. I hate to see drinks go to waste." She ran a finger around the rim of the glass. "If it's okay with you?" Her eyes were more pleading than they needed to be for the half-finished drink.

"Sure," Parn said, and found he had to sit down before he, too, lost his balance.

"Thanks for catching me," she said after the first sip. Then she had a second sip and said, "You're a working man. I can tell."

"What? How do you know?"

She smiled broadly. Red lips and wide white teeth. "Don't worry. Your secret's safe with me. It's the muscles. They're a dead giveaway. Most of the men in here," she leaned back and gestured around the room with a finger, "owe their muscles to stim or the gym. It doesn't make muscles the same." She ran her hand over his forearm, feeling his muscles through the shirt. "My grandpa was a working man. My dad was not. And I could tell the difference. I always know the difference." She smiled and winked.

Not sure what to say, Parn lifted his drink and found it was empty.

"Third one's on me," Saicy said.

"I've already had three."

"Then let me get your fourth." She gestured to Keb to get him another drink. "Now, tell me, what work do you do?"

Parn was relieved, as he just remembered that he probably couldn't actually buy a drink. Ana's tab probably closed when she crossed the threshold. "Me? I'm a corer."

"A corer? In the corer room? How funny. Tell me, how accurate is it?"

"Well, there are no chairs in the trees."

She rolled her eyes at him, then asked, "But what about the scale? Are the trees really this big?"

"Not all of them. I've never been in a tree quite this big, but close. And I know people who have."

Saicy whistled and looked around. "I thought we were making it extra large so we could have the bar in here."

"No, no. They're that big." Parn looked around him and said, "Look, I've got to go find Ana."

"But I just got you a drink. Please, stay to finish it." She put her hand on his. Parn's heart jumped at the smooth warmth of her skin. He swallowed. "Yeah, sure." He said. "But I'll have to drink fast."

"Not so fast that you don't enjoy it." She leaned forward. "Besides, if Ana wants you to find her, she's not going to run away too quickly." She leaned back. "Tell me about her."

"Ana?"

"Who else? Where did you meet her?"

"I met her in Murtoz?" Parn wasn't entirely sure that was the right answer.

"Oh? A beach vacation or a yacht?"

"Actually, a rocket launch."

Saicy scrunched up her face. "I guess they do that there. So you guys are . . . what? Lovers?"

Parn blushed.

"Don't be embarrassed. Just answer."

"Yeah, and . . ." He stopped, unsure how much he should say.

"And?"

"Well, business partners."

"Oh, I see. No wonder you're fighting." She winked. "I'm guessing this visit was business."

"How'd you know?"

"You'd probably pick someplace more comfortable if you were out for fun. What was the purpose of this little excursion?"

Parn had finished his fourth drink and was only too happy to explain, "We wanted to see if I could pass as a professional."

"Are you going to have to talk?"

"No."

"Lemme see you walk."

Parn got up and did his best walk considering his current state.

"Sure, you'll pass," Saicy said.

"But you spotted me right away!"

"Don't let 'em squeeze your biceps and you'll be fine." She squeezed his arm to demonstrate. She looked at Keb, who was visibly impatient. Then she looked back at Parn, "Now, shouldn't you go find Ana?"

"You're right." Parn headed off down the stairs. It was a little bit harder coming down than it had been going up.

He searched the entire lower floor. He didn't find her. After searching for a while, he decided to take a transport pod home. But then he found that they wouldn't take his money. He had more than enough for the trip, but he didn't have credit, so he wasn't cleared for the trip.

He thought about contacting Ana by Tri-I, but he wasn't going to beg her to come get him. He sighed, sat down, and waited.

People came and went. Many of them gave him

a sideways glance. Others pretended he wasn't' there at all. Then, just before closing time, Saicy came out. She was leaning heavily on Keb. At first, Parn thought she was drunk, but then he realized she was just taking her heels off.

She saw Parn. She guessed the problem. "You don't have any credit, do you?"

Parn shook his head.

"Well, come home with me, and I'll get you a ride home in the morning."

Parn hesitated.

"Don't worry. My house has fifteen bedrooms. I'll find a place for you to sleep where you won't bother me."

CHAPTER 9

When Parn woke up, he knew where he was by touch. The bed was too comfortable to be any place he had paid for. Even too comfortable for anything Ana owned or rented. The strange gel in the bed was both soft and hard, responding to his body's needs. It enfolded him but yielded yet supported him when he moved. The sheets were soft and warm. When he opened his eyes, he thought they should be hot with the ambient temperature in the room and the sunlight hitting the bedspread, but he felt perfectly comfortable. He realized the bed was probably reading his stress levels, knowing without being told just how cool he liked to be.

Parn moved to get out of bed, and it got firm, supporting him as he sat up and moved toward the edge. He put his bare feet on the floor and found it, too, was perfectly comfortable. He looked around for his clothes but couldn't find them. He remembered something about a robot shuffling around collecting them as he put them on the floor. Instead, a fresh set of clothes hung near a chair by the door.

Touching the clothes, Parn knew they wouldn't help him pass as a professional. A banker would take one look at these clothes and wonder why he needed funding. The white blouse was so luxuriant that touching it the first time gave him the stirrings of an erection. Putting it on made him so unsteady he had to sit down to recover himself. As he took deep breaths and blinked away the moisture in his eyes, he admired the opalescent colors. He also noticed that the bed had made itself. Afraid of what it might do, Parn didn't put on the new underwear. Instead, once he had recovered, he put on the blue pants. They weren't soft or sensual: they were firm and supportive. They braced his muscles and joints. He knew he'd have a very hard time spraining his knee or ankle in these pants. But they didn't look skin-tight. The outer layer of the fabric stood apart and gave his legs a squared-off appearance.

He found the effect pleasing, although he wasn't too sure about the exaggerated bulge in the crotch. There were no socks or shoes, so he headed out the door barefoot.

When he left the bedroom, the walls disappeared. Though there were at least eight bedrooms and six water closets, the entire floor seemed like one big open area. And halfway across the house on the short axis he saw Saicy. She was looking in a full-length mirror, running her finger along her lips, which blushed lightly at the touch. She wore only a tiny blue thong that split and defined her round butt. He looked at her reflection. Her big breasts hung down heavily, with tan lines scooping just over the pert, light brown nipples. Saicy caught his eyes in the reflection. Parn felt himself redden.

Then she winked at him and smiled. He was no longer embarrassed, just full of desire. But it was not the kind of desire that made him want to rush to her. It was more like a divine awe that held him rooted to the spot. He could not possibly move. He couldn't take a step. He couldn't touch himself. He couldn't even close his slack jaw.

Still smiling, Saicy turned around and gave him

the full frontal view. She tilted her hips, which made her breasts and the slight paunch of her stomach bounce. Then she made a sharp gesture and the walls solidified around her.

The spell broken, Parn looked around to find the stairs. He didn't remember much about the house, only that he was on the second floor. He could see the top of the stairs and headed toward them. He noticed that the walls gained a slight opacity as he approached them, just enough to hint they were there. And the closer he got, the more solid they became. The stairs were solid as he went down them, but once he reached the bottom, only the top and bottom three steps were visible.

It was easy to see the kitchen, and he headed toward it. Parn sat down in a chair near the outer wall—the open area was starting to get to him. He was happy to note that when he leaned back in the chair, the interior wall solidified, showing that his seat was in a corner.

After a few moments, a quiet synthetic voice asked, "Would you like breakfast or something to drink?"

Parn said, "I feel like I could use a whiskey." He was still trembling a little.

The voice replied, "Guests in this house are not served alcohol before lunch without authorization from the hostess. Should I ask her if you are allowed whiskey at this time?"

"No, no. That's okay."

"Perhaps you would like something caffeinated? Coffee, tea, and kzlek are all compatible with your physiology. I can also add caffeine to a fruit juice or other beverage of your choice."

"Coffee would be fine."

"I can add cream, sugar, and spices or bring them to the table."

"Just black and strong will do fine."

"Very well. Breakfast?"

"Coffee first."

The coffee machine whirred to life. Then a serving robot took the coffee cup to him. The robot had long, slender legs and arms, a small body with an even smaller sensory complex designed to give the impression of a face. Its proportions reminded him of an arboreal primate like a gibbon, though it moved smoothly with complete assurance on the flat kitchen floor. Parn sipped the coffee. Stronger than he was used to, but it was as delicious as it was bracing.

As Parn was finishing his first cup and contemplating a second, Saicy came down the stairs. He noticed the movement out of the corner of his eye and initially panicked at the thing coming toward him from above and behind. Then he turned and saw it was a foot. The foot was shapely and tapered, resting lightly on the ball and toes before lifting to pass its partner on the steps that were appearing beneath them.

He followed the foot up to a curvaceous calf, a luscious thigh, and a pair of wide, swinging hips, all covered in a close-fitting material. Her top hung loose over her stomach, and as she descended, it billowed outward, revealing the smooth lightly tanned skin of her midriff. Parn's eyes skipped guiltily up to Saicy's face. He saw that she was watching him with a smile, and he turned quickly back to his coffee.

As she came around the corner, the robot met her with a beverage. She sat down as the kitchen whirred to life, starting to slice, blend, and cook numerous items, presumably for her benefit. Parn could only look at her through the corner of his eye, but that was enough to notice that the shirt, which was loose around her belly, was tight around her breasts, formfitting over her mounds and erect nipples.

"How are you feeling, dear?" she asked. Her voice had an unusual accent that hadn't been present last night and never showed up in her movies. It gave him a feeling of intimacy even greater than seeing her almost naked.

"Fine," Parn replied.

"Did you get breakfast? It doesn't look like you've had anything to eat."

"No, no. I haven't."

"You should eat something. Soon."

"Why?" Parn didn't dare ask directly if she was planning on throwing him out. He had a strong suspicion.

"Otherwise you're likely to forget." A robot placed a dish in front of her. Parn couldn't identify most of it by sight: just the sliced fruit on one side. His nostrils recognized that there was probably some animal protein in there somewhere, but he couldn't be sure what. "Things are going to move quickly."

"No, I'm okay. Maybe just a second cup of coffee." The robot moved quickly to take his cup.

"I'd advise against that," Saicy said. "You don't

want to spend your morning peeing. It will be inconvenient."

The robot had stopped the instant Saicy said "against," its hand just centimeters from Parn's mug.

Saicy gestured dismissively with her fork. "I just said 'advise.' He can have another cup if he wants."

"Yes, hostess," the robot said and took Parn's cup.

"Uh, on second thought," Parn said, "maybe not."

"If you want," the robot said. It took his mug and put it in a receptacle in the kitchen.

Parn turned toward Saicy, looked at her plate. She dug in quickly to the hearty main dish, shoveling large forkfuls in through her red lips. After she finished this dish, she moved on to the fruits, picking pieces up with her fingers.

"Hostess," the robot said, "I hate to interrupt, but there is a woman at the gate."

"Perfect," Saicy said to the robot. "Let her in." Then she turned to Parn. "That will be your Ana."

"What?" Parn said. "How'd she know I'm here?"

"I told her."

"Wait—how? How did you know who she was?"

Saicy finished the last piece of fruit then stood up. The robot whisked the plate away just as the piece of fruit was lifted off it. "It's my business to know people." She smiled and swiveled her hips, making her breasts bounce. "What, did you think I got by on my looks alone?"

He didn't respond, but he couldn't help looking her up and down. She laughed.

Ana came in the room led by a robot that Parn initially thought was the same as the kitchen robot, but then he caught that one in his peripheral vision, tidying up the cooking spaces with the help of several built-in kitchen arms. She came right up to Parn, as close as if she might hug him, but her anger drove like a wave in front of her, and Parn took a step back. "What were you thinking, going home with this woman?" She didn't step forward: she filled the space between them with an angry pointing finger.

Parn prickled, "I was thinking I had been left behind in that godforsaken icy waste. I was thinking I had no way home. I was thinking I would have to walk to the nearest transit site—assuming the police didn't pick me up first for vagrancy." The very thought made Parn angrier. It stung that all the money he'd earned as a corer was tossed aside because he didn't have credit.

"Oh, as if that wasn't what you were wishing for, anyway. God, the way you eyed her as soon as she came in the room!"

Parn couldn't help his eyes dashing over to Saicy leaning against the kitchen island, accepting a refill from the kitchen robot.

"You are insufferable!" Ana said. "I pull you off the street, help you look for investors, get you some decent clothes, and then as soon as you see her, you're ready to throw me away." Her voice was still full of anger, but the corners of her mouth were curving and quivering as if she might cry. Her arm trembled, the finger still outstretched but wavering.

Parn wanted to say, "First of all, you didn't pick me up off the street. I was on the run, and, yeah, I was looking for help, but I wasn't destitute like you think. Second of all, don't act like you didn't get what you wanted out of me—practically stole it from me while I slept!" But he didn't say anything for a moment. Then he reached out and touched her shoulder gently. Her finger sank down at her side, and her face contorted as she tried to hold in a sob. She looked away. Now he pulled her close in what he hoped was a comforting embrace. He did say, "Don't ever think that I want to throw you away. I want you close, like this, all the time."

For a moment, Ana seemed stilled, but then she pushed out of his embrace, "But you came home with her! You slept with her!" Now Ana's finger pointed angrily at Saicy.

Saicy stood up from her releaxed position. Her lips were now very close to the tip of Ana's finger. "Excuse me," she said, "but let me clarify." She enunciated almost as if she meant to bite off Ana's finger.

Ana turned and looked at Saicy, giving her a withering look.

Saicy was unaffected. She continued, "He may have slept in my house, but there are fifteen bedrooms here. He slept on the opposite side of the house."

"It's true," Parn said, thinking it appropriate not to mention the often-transparent walls.

Ana looked back at Parn. "You didn't sleep in her bed? Didn't kiss her? Didn't caress her?"

Parn was slow in response. Saicy was not. She laughed.

"Caress me?" She walked closer to Parn. Parn watched her move. "He can't even touch me." She leaned in, and he shied away as if she were made of fire. "See? He's a little darling." She put her mug down on the end of the island, did a little turn, and let herself fall into a chair. "There's no doubt he worships me, but he's scared of me, too. You have no worries on that score."

Ana was quiet. She looked back and forth between the two of them.

Saicy said, "As enjoyable as this little scene is, I called you here for business, not pleasure."

"And what business could we possibly have with you?" Ana asked.

"If I'm completely honest," Saicy said, looking down at the table, "I'm not entirely sure. But let me tell you what I know," she looked up at them with her eyes, her head still tilted downward. Parn swooned a little. Ana bristled. "He's a corer. You're a navigator. He described your visit to my little hole last night as business. That's what I know. Anything you care to dispute?"

Ana stepped forward. She was now between

Saicy and Parn. "No. That's correct. But just because we took our business to your club doesn't mean that it concerns you."

Saicy raised her head and looked at Ana with her full face. She smiled and waved dismissively. "Maybe not. But let me tell you what I suspect. The only business that brings navigators and corers together is a pepper planet. And if you're trying to make him look professional, that probably means you're trying to get funding, right?"

Ana didn't confirm or object. She motioned for Saicy to continue.

"And what do you need funding for? You could be trying to buy some property together, but, looking at you two, I guess you're not at that point yet." Saicy looked between the two of them, read their response and continued, "So what you probably need funding for is a pepper expedition."

"That's pretty unlikely, isn't it?" Ana said. She put one hand on her hip and with the other hand, she made a motion as if casting the idea aside. "I mean what are the odds that a corer would know the location of an unexploited pepper planet?"

"I know, pretty unlikely, huh?" Saicy rolled her eyes. "But if he did, and if you, as a navigator," she pointed at Ana, "confirmed the viability of that location, it would be very lucky for all of us. You see, I've long been looking for an investment opportunity just like this one. I've tried to sniff out a few through my regular investment brokers, but every time I find one, my brand manager steps in and breaks up the deal because he says it's not good for my image. So if you guys have just such an opportunity for me, I would jump at the chance."

"But wouldn't your brand manager object to such an investment?"

"Oh, yes, but it won't matter. He has influence over my brokers," she gestured at the empty table, then at herself, "but not over me. And not," she leaned forward and pointed with two fingers on one hand, "over you." She paused. Taking the silence as assent, she leaned back in the seat. "So, if I'm right, let's get started on this right away. The more we can get done before my brand manager finds out, the less he can interfere."

"I thought you said he didn't have influence over you?"

"No, but I don't keep all my assets in my pockets," she stretched out a leg and gestured to show that there was no room in her skin-fitting clothes for pockets, let alone all her assets. Though a good many of them were there, to be sure. "He can block some of them. There are so many contracts I had to sign—you have no idea!"

"But wait," Parn said, "why would you want to do something that could jeopardize your image?"

"How gallant of you to be concerned," Saicy said. "But it's not a serious worry. My earnings might take a hit, sure, but it's the kind of thing that mostly looks bad on an investor spreadsheet. It won't affect me at all. I may have to take some lesser roles for a while, but, if we play it right, I may be doing better when we get back than I am now."

"Woah, wait," Parn said. "When we get back? You're not coming with us!"

"So there is an expedition?"

Ana looked angrily over her shoulder at Parn. He sighed. "Yes. That's the hope, at least, if we can find an investor."

"That's great!" Saicy bounced up out of her chair. "You've found one, but my condition is that I have to come along."

"Why would you want that?" Ana asked, suspicious.

"Because I'm so in love with the pepper trade.

That's why I themed Heliopause that way. I've wanted to go along on an expedition like this for nearly all my life. You have no idea. Just let me come, and I'll pay for all of it! I'll even pay the crew work-for-hire rates so you don't have to offer them shares. And, speaking of shares, you two can have 75%, and I'll just take 25. You know you won't get that kind of offer from a bank."

Ana had told him the kind of deal they could expect from a bank. She glanced at Parn, who was now working hard to keep his mouth shut. He was deferring to her on this. "Let me look at the contract," she said slowly.

"Great!" Saicy said. She jumped up in the air. "My robot has it all ready for you to evaluate. Cap, send them the contract!"

CHAPTER 10

Saicy wanted to work fast. The robot had generated three versions of the contract: one for each of them. They specified the breakdown of shares. In return for her investment covering the full cost of the first expedition, Saicy was guaranteed one quarter of the gross revenue from the first cargo and an equivalent share of any future cargoes from the same starsystem. She was not, however, required to spend the full cost of any subsequent trips to and from the starsystem: she was allowed to negotiate a division of transport expenses without relinquishing her claim to the full quarter of the gross. In addition, she got all media rights to any entertainments and documentaries about this or future trips.

She left the final hiring decisions on crew to

Parn, but the contract stipulated that she would not pay any wage that was more than 25% over the median for any position. If crew were to be offered shares, it would not come from Saicy's 25%. Parn had final decision over how the other 75% would be divided up, although he could not give Ana less than 25%.

This much Parn could understand. Much of the rest of it was unclear to him.

Ana read the entire contract through. Parn watched her face as she read. Initially hard, it softened as she read. By the end, she was smiling, but she suppressed her smile before speaking. "It seems fair. I'm glad to see you didn't try to indemnify us for your potential losses on this expedition beyond your initial investment. Including your life or your brand, not even your face!"

Saicy took another sip from her coffee and leaned backward, smiling. "It's my choice, so it's my risk. Besides, you guys are already putting everything you have into this expedition. Trying to get anything more out of you would be like squeezing spit from the sun."

Parn thought that he would never forgive himself if anything happened to Saicy's face. But he also worried about certifying a contract he didn't understand. He said to Ana, "Can we talk before certifying?"

Ana nodded, then looked at Saicy, who made a dismissive gesture. The two of them walked out of the kitchen. They were in a room clearly designed for comfortable entertaining. Despite the transparency of the walls, it felt like a truly separate space, defined by deep carpet and a luxurious sofa pit. They didn't enter the pit but walked far enough that they didn't think Saicy would hear them. Parn didn't know the command to make the wall turn solid, so he put his hand on it. The area he touched turned opaque, and he felt this was enough to block Saicy from reading their lips.

Parn said, "I don't understand most of the contract. What do you think about it?"

"I'm about ready to certify it," Ana replied. "She's right: the terms are better than we'd have gotten at any of the banks. I've looked over a lot of contracts, and I've never seen anything as favorable as this. She even guarantees me the rights to calculating the new transit lanes."

"Maybe the terms are too good," Parn said. "Can we trust her?"

Ana shook her head. "Personally, I don't trust that chubby ewe any further than I could throw her. But I don't have to. I can trust the contract. And it's all there. It's all there. We're even protected if we decide to back out of the contract in the future."

Parn was still worried about losing what Vigar had trusted to him. "What about the navigation crystal? Could she be using this as a ploy to get the crystal from us?"

Ana shook her head again. "She never gets it. Before she certifies, she gets to look at the certification crystal data, the same as we showed to the bankers. Then you release the data to the navigator. The crystal stays in your possession. Nobody else gets to see it."

Parn took a deep breath. Then he took another. "Okay, let's go certify."

Ana smiled and hugged Parn. "This is the right decision. We will never get another opportunity like this!"

Parn nodded. He was still unsure. Ana led him back into the kitchen. When Saicy saw them, she smiled. "Ready to certify?"

Parn nodded. Ana said, "Before I certify, I wonder why you didn't have a human lawyer draw this up for us?"

Saicy's smile vanished. Her lips were still curved. Her teeth were still showing. Some people might have mistaken it for a smile, but all the happiness had gone out of it. "People have their own agendas. Robots just do what I tell them to."

Parn burst out spontaneously, "That's why, uh, Keb, isn't here?"

Saicy nodded. "Keb is my brand manager's creature. He's a public accessory—and a thoroughgoing nuisance." She noticed that neither Ana nor Parn had certified the contract. "Don't worry—the language is all standard modules. It'll hold up in court, if that's your hesitation."

"No worry," Ana said. "I recognized a lot of the legal modules. This is similar to a contract I might have put together. Just curious." She certified the contract. Seeing that Ana certified the contract, Parn did, too. The robot verified his identity in the 20 different ways required by the United Market Covenant on Contract Certification.

"Great," Saicy said, "now we can start finding our crew. Looks like the legal minimum for a human crewed pepper expedition is seven. We need to have one primary pilot who can perform an un-aided takeoff and landing. We also need a secondary pilot who can perform an unaided landing. We need a navigator capable of both in-system navigation and Rho Space plots." Saicy looked up at Ana. "Is that you?"

"Yes, I can do Rho Space plots, if that's what you're asking."

"Good. We need a person with basic medical certification. And an engineer who can monitor and tune the fusion drives. Plus, we need two corers and two core certification robots. And we can only sell pepper if the robots certify it. So we need to make sure the robots weigh everything—and protect their memories. We can mix and match skills, but we still need seven people." She made some deft motions in the air with her hand and said, "Now I'll just post this to the top job boards, and we should be able to start interviewing candidates this afternoon."

"You can't do that," Parn said.

"What?"

"Posting to the job boards. It doesn't work."

"Thanks for the advice, partner, but I've chartered dozens of ships—I know how the process goes."

"It's different for pepper ships, though." Parn stopped at the look that Saicy gave him. He couldn't keep talking while looking into those big, brown eyes that could be so soft but had suddenly turned hard. He looked away. "See, most of the people who work the pepper—the ones who know what they're doing—they know those boards are bogus. We tell all the stories all the time. Everybody knows somebody who's been taken in by one of those scams.

"So nobody with any experience will sign onto a job unless it's vouched for by someone they know. If we want to sign on a good crew, we have to go to the port ourselves."

"Parn," Ana broke in, "I thought you couldn't go to the docks. What about Astreyan?"

"I know, but I have to go anyway."

Saicy looked from the one to the other. "Who's Astreyan?"

Parn was quiet.

Saicy looked at Ana.

Ana made a gesture to communicate that she

was skipping details. "Astreyan wants to kill Parn and take the navigation data."

"Well, he won't do that now. I've got a stake in the data and a contract."

Ana said, "Things happen at the docks. We don't know the details. But sometimes we prep an expedition, and the contract gets lost."

"Contracts get lost all the time. Maybe they got a better bid."

"No, see," Ana looked from Saicy to Parn and back. "Sometimes there's a crew member we're used to working with—a captain, onboard navigator, even a core wrangler—and then this contract goes missing and their name doesn't show up again."

Saicy gave a half smile and said, "That sounds like a bunch of office gossip."

"No," Parn said, "it does happen. It's rare, but it happens."

Saicy looked at Parn for a moment. "Maybe so, but I'll make sure nothing happens. You'll be safe with me."

"You don't know what you're getting into."

"No," Saicy said, "the port don't know what's coming." She patted her lap with both hands and sprang to her feet. "Now, all this talk about pepper is making me hungry. Let's eat before we go. I don't know how you two can just talk about pepper so casually without getting the munchies." She looked at the two of them and suddenly she froze. "Wait—" she said, pointing at Parn, "you've never had star pepper, have you?"

"Not as food," Parn said. "You have to taste it to make sure it's ripe."

"But you've never actually eaten a dish seasoned with it?" Saicy's smile got really big—the largest, most genuine smile Parn had seen from her. "What a delightful irony! And a perfect way to celebrate. Ana, what's your favorite pepper dish?"

Ana looked down and colored.

"No? You've never tried it?"

To Parn's surprise, Ana didn't look up. Her shoulders heaved in a big sigh, and Parn could see her fists clenched under the table. Tears welled in the corners of her eyes. Parn didn't understand and didn't know what to do, but Saicy swept down and wrapped her arms around Ana. Ana's body shivered once, and Saicy tightened her grip until the shivering stopped.

Saicy kissed Ana on the cheek and let her go.

The two women looked each other in the eye, then Saicy stood up. "That settles it. Cap, convert the kitchen. I'm cooking!"

The main kitchen robot said, "Your brand protection contract explicitly forbids you from cooking. Brand-damaging injuries may result. Even if you are not injured, you may be fined."

Saicy blew a raspberry. "I know, now just convert the damn kitchen."

The robot deferred. "Of course, hostess. I am legally obligated to mention this provision, even though I knew you would defy it."

The kitchen changed slightly, with robots moving away from the countertops and cooking surfaces becoming exposed. Saicy selected a recipe with a few quick movements of her finger, and robots set about preparing some of the ingredients. After a while, she turned around to Parn and Ana who had been sitting awkwardly at the table. She held up a small vial. "It's time to put in the lucky ingredient." She raised the vial high. "Here's to a successful voyage."

Parn sank back in his chair. He almost fell out of it. He had never seen star pepper in quantities smaller than the half-kilo chunks he cut out of the trees. He looked around the mansion, with its numerous rooms, technologies, and conveniences. The bed and clothes comfortable beyond his wildest dreams. He thought about Saicy's status as an interstellar entertainment personality. He realized that the small vial was proportionate to her wealth and celebrity.

And for the first time in his life, Parn realized the true value of star pepper.

When Saicy brought the plates to the table, the dish didn't look like much. The purplish tubers gleamed with a brown caramelized sauce. Parn didn't recognize the diced pungent vegetables that were mixed in. The smell coming off the plate was sweet, savory, and sour, laced with the unmistakable terpenoid aroma of star pepper. Parn was prepared for the burn, but it was much less than he was used to. What he wasn't prepared for was the complex array of flavors that splashed across his tongue. There was the tuber and the pungent vegetables, but the electric undercurrent that energized them all was star pepper. He made an involuntary sound of pleasure. Then he pressed his tongue against his palate to magnify and, he hoped, freeze the flavors there on his tongue. But they invariably faded as he chewed and swallowed. So he took another bite.

Saicy smiled at Parn, her deeply dimpled cheeks blushing slightly. "I know, it's so good! I'm not much of a cook, but in this dish, the ingredients do all the work. I just throw them together and cook 'em a little."

Parn nodded, then looked at Ana, who hadn't had any yet. She had turned her head away. The smell was obviously bothering her. She looked at Parn for reassurance.

"Go ahead and try it," Parn said. "It's delicious!"

Ana's eyebrows betrayed her doubt, but she turned back to the dish, speared a tuber, and put it into her mouth. No sooner had she closed her mouth than she opened it again and began panting. "Shit, that's hot!"

"Oh, oh, yeah, if you're not used to it. Cap, a drink!"

The robot sprang to life. "What kind of drink, hostess?"

Saicy looked at Ana, who said, "Anything to kill this heat!"

A second robot brought a glass to the first. Cap

put the milky, translucent liquid in front of Ana, who guzzled it.

"Not a fan?" Saicy asked, frowning a little.

"I dunno—I couldn't taste anything for the heat! I'll try another bite."

"Atta girl," Saicy said. "Cap, bring her another drink, and one for me, too."

Saicy went and served herself what remained in the pan. While her back was turned, Ana leaned over to Parn and said, "Taste mine: I think she's trying to poison me!"

Parn quickly scooped up some of the vegetables. He put it in his mouth. It tasted the same as his. But since Saicy was coming back to the table, Parn didn't know how to tell Ana this, so he just said, "Mmm," and shrugged subtly.

Saicy sat down and began to eat. Parn ended up eating most of Ana's food, and she thanked him. Since she didn't eat much, Saicy let Ana raid her cabinets to make her own lunch. Then when she finished eating, Saicy excused herselt to get ready to go to the port. Parn had no conception of what she planned to bring with her.

CHAPTER 11

They went to the port as Parn requested, but Saicy insisted they use a special cargo car that ran below and apart from the passenger rails. Ana argued that she shouldn't go.

Parn replied, "But I need you there."

Ana turned away from him. "I don't know anything about the port, and I won't do you any good there."

Parn shrugged. "Maybe you don't know anything about the port, but you know contracts. If you don't come, I'll be at the mercy of Saicy and her robots."

"You at the mercy of Saicy? I don't want that, though I don't see what I can do to help it." She smiled as she turned back and punched Parn lightly.

Parn looked away. "Some things just can't be helped."

"But her contracts seem fair. More than fair, really. Her profit margin on this pepper cargo has got to be paper thin."

"Should we be suspicious?"

Ana bobbed her head from side to side. "Maybe. But the exit terms on the contract are more than fair, too. There are no punitive terms. We can walk away at any time and never look back—there's no downside."

Parn said, "See, I need you there because I don't know any of this. And we're going to be making contracts for all the new crew members."

Ana took a deep sigh. "But it's the port. Stuff happens there. It's dangerous."

Parn put his hand on Ana's. "Saicy blew off your fears about the port, but you're right. It can be dangerous. But I know the dangers. I've spent my life avoiding them. If you trust me and follow my lead, you'll avoid them, too. Okay?"

Ana pursed her lips. She nodded.

When they reached the station at the edge of the port, Parn and Ana climbed out of the train. Saicy climbed into her combat mecha. It was about four meters tall and bright pink. It was bipedal, though its legs were jointed like a bird's rather than a human's. The arms ended in manipulators and weapons, which further reduced its similarity to human shape. It had the company logo in baby blue on it, as well as Saicy's serpentine signature in a darker blue. "It's one of my biggest endorsements," Saicy explained. "My audience loves it. When I fire the guns, the recoil gives me a great bounce!"

Parn could easily imagine, but as pleasant as the thought was, he wasn't happy with having the monstrous machine accompany him into the port. Saicy strapped herself in, closed the wide transparent canopy, then activated the device. It stood up, and even with that little motion, Parn saw that the wide canopy gave ample view of the bounce provided by the machine. The mecha daintily stepped out of the cargo car. Ana and Parn crowded off to one side of the elevator, but the machine seemed to know where they were and gave them a wide margin.

When they reached street level, Saicy's mecha attracted a lot of attention. People pointed at it, took images, even launched camera drones. Saicy immediately became her public self. She blew kisses, waved, and shimmied her short skirt to the extent that she could in the safety harness. She even made the mecha do a slight jump to give her fans a little bounce. Parn noticed how surprisingly light on its feet the machine was. There was a lot of power in the takeoff and landing, but the segmented toes curled to absorb the shock. It could probably stalk along as quietly as a cat if the driver wanted it to.

With three faint "poofs," the mecha launched tiny camera drones. "In case they pick up some usable commercial footage. I have a feeling that this is one endorsement that won't be affected by brand changes on this expedition." She winked. "Oh, and for security" Saicy added. "It never hurts to have a few extra cameras running."

Parn didn't know how to respond to all the attention. He was surprised when Ana grabbed his left hand in her right. He felt a tremble in her palm. He looked at her and saw that she was terrified. He remembered her stories about the port and realized that he couldn't show uncertainty here. Ana depended on him for his confidence when she was so out of her element.

He thought about kissing her hand or giving her a hug. As comforting as those might be, they didn't feel right for the port environment. Instead, he disentangled his hand from hers. He put his hand on her shoulder and gave it a slight squeeze. He looked her in the eye and tried his best to look strong and certain. Then he said, "C'mon. If we leave the pace up to Saicy, she'll waste the entire day soaking up the attention."

He walked between the legs of the mecha and toward the entrance to the port district. The scanners thoroughly inspected their records, but the guards let him and Ana through with but a glance. On the other side of the gate, Ana took his hand again.

But as Saicy approached the gate, the guards came to attention, several cannons trained on the mecha, and Parn expected unseen weapons did, too. One of the guards called out, "Open your canopy and declare yourself."

The mecha crouched. The canopy opened. "Why, dear," Saicy said, "surely you recognize *me*."

She put on the moves, batting her eyes, pouting her lips, tilting her head, and swinging her hips. The guard looked close enough to human that it might have worked. But it didn't. He gave her a stern look and gestured again for the declaration. She must have sent it because he started to look over his coms.

"I have a permit to go in," she said as she pointed.

The guard looked it over. "So you do. But permit or no, it gets pretty narrow and crowded in there. Use caution." Then he gestured, and the gate opened for her mecha.

Saicy came over to where Parn and Ana waited. Then Parn resumed walking.

Fewer people gawked inside. Everyone noticed the machine—it was too big and too pink to miss—but they were just as likely to feign indifference as to stop and stare. The mecha picked its way through the crowd, demonstrating even more daintiness than Parn had suspected.

Parn led them through the crowd toward the neighborhood where humans gathered when they were looking for work. The air was close, with human smells mixed with alcohol and machine oil. Most walked, but a few rode noisy scooters that people dodged more vigorously than they did the mecha.

After a while, Saicy said, "Hold on."

Parn turned around. He let go of Ana's hand. The problem was clear: there were too many things strung across the street for her mecha to get through. Transmission wires, clothes lines, advertising banners, and more were becoming too frequent for the mecha to duck under or hop over. Saicy pulled it off to the side of the street next to a pile of refuse. She opened the canopy and extended the ladder down. Once she was on the ground, she made some gestures at the mecha.

As she was putting on her heels, a hatch on the near side of the mecha opened, lowering a humanoid robot, also painted pink with the distinct blue signature on it, but with a different company logo emblazoned on the chest. A second came from the opposite side. Saicy tasked one of the drones to observe the mecha, which locked down, compressing all its joints and clamping a shield over its canopy. A short time later, they heard the mecha warning passersby to keep their distance as it had entered sentry mode.

Parn didn't wait for Saicy to catch up. He put his hand on Ana's back and guided her through the crowd toward the entrance of a bar. Inside, the air was thick and musky. Parn knew from experience that the dominant smell gave way in the corners to a sour, rotten odor. And if you looked in those corners, you would see a little wedge of blood that cheap floor cleaning robot couldn't reach. But Parn hoped to stay out of the corners.

He scanned the bar for people he knew. He saw only one. Parn headed to his table. "Rafe," he said, "let's have a drink." Rafe happily agreed. Parn guided Ana to a seat and then sat. He interfaced with the bar computer and ordered a bottle with five glasses.

"How you been, Rafe?" Parn asked.

"Not my best, that's for sure," Rafe said. "Work seems like hell until you get to retirement. That's worse."

"You're retired? What're you doing here, then?" Parn gestured vaguely.

"Semi-retired. I lost my primary pilot's license. I was so mad. I didn't want to be second on anyone's ship, at first." A simple automated server arrived with the bottle of vodka made from the local tuber and faintly purple. Parn assumed the color was artificial, and it wasn't his favorite, but he remembered that Rafe liked it.

Not being able to work too often with the same people meant that every spacer maintained a complex mental database of all the people he'd met. You usually hooked up with someone for security and amusement early in the voyage. The long travel times to and from jumps could lead to some strong friendships. You relied on these people when you were in port, and counted on them for recommendations for food, brothels, and, of course, work.

Parn poured a glass for Rafe, one for himself, and one for Ana. Saicy was just arriving at the table, the two pink robots behind her looking even brighter inside, not just because of their paint, but because the complicated instrument cluster on their head lit up in dozens of colors. Parn raised a glass in question. She looked at the label and snorted, "Why not?" She took it from his hand.

Parn raised his glass. "To old friends . . . and new." Parn, Rafe, and Saicy downed their liquor in a single gulp. Ana sipped. Without asking, Parn poured a new glass for himself and Rafe. He then moved the bottle toward Saicy's glass. She had her lips pursed and her face was turning red. "That's sharp," she croaked. She cleared her throat. "I've had this brand before—I insisted on tasting every drink we stocked at Heliopause. But I forgot how sharp it is. I'll get something else next time."

Parn put the bottle down. The burn that still lingered in his throat just seemed normal. It was easing off as he and Rafe began sipping their second glass.

"Speaking of new friends . . . who are they?"

Parn gestured. "This is Ana, a navigator. And this is Saicy, an investor."

Rafe's smile got wide, and his eyes gogged at Saicy. "Fer real?"

Saicy raised her left hand, tilting her head and shoulders to make a dramatic shape and said with fluttering eyelids, "In the flesh!"

Rafe laughed. "I thought you looked like her but I couldn't believe it. There've been some wild rumors going around about you, Parn, but nothing saying you were mixed up with a vid star!" He pointed at parn with his left hand around his glass. "So do you have a stolen map?"

"It's not stolen. Vigar gave it to me."

"You two were close. I can believe it. But I dunno about the rest of these guys." He gestured vaguely with the quarter-full glass. "I think they're more likely to believe Astreyan . . . or his money."

"I don't need the rest of them to believe me. I just need a crew that believes."

"And what if one of them decides to take a shot at you for the money?"

Saicy broke in, "That's why I'm here. As a bodyguard."

Rafe looked at her. "I thought you were an investor."

"I guess you could say I have a lot of assets." Saicy brought her arms close to her sides and lifted her bosom up as she looked sheepishly away. Then she gestured with a luxuriant hand at the robot on her left. "These are the latest model personal protection robots from Xantseco! I don't go anywhere without them, and I feel completely safe. I've let them know to protect Parn and Ana, too." She leaned forward and whispered, "It's a new promotional contract. I dunno how long I'll keep it, but for now the robots are a nice benefit."

Parn gestured to get back Rafe's attention. The man's eyes kept lingering on Saicy. Parn knew she could be distracting and wanted to get the conversation back on track. When Rafe looked back—a little slowly, it's true—Parn said, "We're looking for a pilot, Rafe."

"Oh, I can be your pilot!" He gestured at himself with his glass.

"I thought you said you were retired."

"Well, officially, but I can still pilot. I'm really as sharp as I ever was."

Saicy said, "We need a legal pilot. I'm exposed here."

Rafe looked at her quickly.

"Financially, I mean. The insurance won't cover the expedition unless it's properly crewed. That means a licensed primary pilot. You can be secondary."

Rafe looked back at Parn with a questioning expression.

Parn shrugged. "She writes the checks, she calls the shots. I'm here to tell you that this game is square. This is not an opportunity you want to miss. If you come on this expedition, you will be able to buy yourself a ship when you get back. Then you can get reclassed with a PrivPiL and fly your own ship all you want. But if she says you can't be primary on this expedition, then you can't be primary. Now the question is: can you direct us to a primary pilot who will work with you as secondary?"

Rafe slugged the rest of his liquor, then put his glass down for more. He clenched his jaw and ground his teeth. Parn poured him another glass. "A lot of my class has retired. Really retired, I mean." Parn could tell from his tone that Rafe didn't really want to fly, but he was broke and needed the work. "There's this kid, Urgot, though. He was my secondary when he was learning to fly. I've crewed with him a few times. He's good. Trustworthy, too."

"Okay," Parn said. He sipped his vodka. "You get in touch with him and tell him you've got an opportunity for him as a contract primary . . . if he'll work with you as secondary."

Rafe looked off into space, tapping his left wrist.

Ana tapped Parn on the wrist. He saw her message: "Are you sure this is the right way to do this?"

Parn shrugged and messaged back, "This is the way I was recruited for noncorp jobs."

"But a pilot?"

Parn stiffened, then replied, "A corer is as skilled a professional as a pilot. More so—a pilot lets the computer fly, but a corer cuts the pepper with his own hands."

"Fine."

Parn looked around the room more carefully. He saw a few more faces he recognized, but none that stood out. Some looked over at him hopefully. They sensed that something was up, and they wanted in on the action.

When Rafe refocused his eyes on Parn, he said, "Urgot should be on his way here."

Parn went to the bar to get another glass, taking advantage of the opportunity to better scrutinize the patrons. "I don't see a lot of familiar faces here," Parn said when he returned.

"Bad timing. They rousted the crews for several corporate ships yesterday."

"Hmmm . . . I'd like to get at least one more person I really feel comfortable with. What about Mehany?"

"She was here, but I think she contracted yesterday. She won't have left yet. You might be able to talk to her, if you hurry."

"If she's already contracted, what's the point?"

Ana broke in, leaning forward and pointing assertively. "Well, it would be possible to buy her out of her contract, if you really want her. Is she another pilot?"

"No, she's a corer."

"Oh," Ana said and leaned back.

"We still need a second corer, though," Parn said. He looked over the faces again. Then one of them caught his eye. He got up and walked over to a booth where a man was playing a video game projected onto the table. "Hey," he said, "you're Seldon, right?"

The man's tanned face turned slowly. "Seldon," he said, but his eyes seemed like they hadn't fully transitioned out of his game world.

"I'm Parnassus Jackson. We crewed together about five years ago. You're a corer, right? A good one, if I remember."

Seldon scratched his chin, fingers abrading loudly on his stubble. "Maybe I remember you. I keep above grade. Never missed a share, so I guess that makes me a pretty good corer."

"It just so happens I'm looking for a corer. Are you free to ship out?"

After a little more discussion, Seldon agreed, and Parn gestured for Saicy's contract robot to come over. Seldon signed on for a small share. Then Parn sauntered back to the central table with the robot.

"Hey," Rafe said before Parn had even reached the table, "you find a medic, yet?"

"No. Who you have in mind?"

"Mamillo."

"Mellow Mamillo? He's still around?"

"Yeah. Oh, yeah! He's working at Merkellis. I mean, he was. It's possible they rousted him."

"Of course. Let's head over there after Urgot gets here."

Rafe waved his hand. "No need. I'll just let him know we're looking for him and have him come here." Rafe stared off into space for a moment. "No, no. He's not responding."

"He has a com, but he almost never uses it."

"Right. Hey, here's Urgot now."

With the light behind him, Parn couldn't pick up much more than the man's shape—slender—or the way he moved—smooth, like an automaton whose core motion might be gears and cogs, but whose limbs were just held on by pins at well-lubricated joints.

As Urgot walked around the table the long way to sit next to Saicy, Parn caught sight of Ana's face. She looked deeply suspicious. Of course she would be, Parn thought. She was suspicious of this whole process.

For himself, Parn withheld judgment until the man sat down and he could see his entire face. And when he saw the face, Parn had to admit that he wasn't sure he liked what he saw. Urgot's hair was held firmly in place and had an oily sheen. His smile was slippery, and his glance slid over everything. Even when he spent too much time checking Saicy out, his eyes were never still: they just oozed over and over the same places. Parn glanced over at Rafe, who smiled, grunted "Huh?" and gestured at Urgot.

Ana spoke first, "So you're a pilot?"

"Yes, ma'am. I'm a great pilot. Not a single incident on my record."

Saicy asked, "A licensed pilot? Fully bonded?"

"Yes, ma'am. You can check my license. It's all in order. Primary pilot certified. I've headed up more'n a dozen corporate missions."

Saicy held up her arm. "Show me."

Urgot moved to touch his wrist against hers, but Saicy was very skilled at Tri-I transfers. She kept their arms just close enough that the data was transferred without actually touching. Parn saw him jerk his arm forward suddenly to try to catch her, but her movements were too quick and deft for that to work. Urgot was visibly disappointed.

To distract him, Parn slid a glass to Urgot. Then he raised the bottle and poured. He didn't ask for confirmation from anyone but poured full glasses all around. He knew Rafe would happily finish whatever didn't get drunk.

Saicy said, "Well your license and record check out. Completely clean, just like you said."

Rafe raised his glass and said, "To successful ventures!" They all drank. Ana coughed.

"Speaking of ventures," Urgot said, "Rafe didn't tell me much about this one. Can you fill me in?"

Parn looked over at Ana and Saicy, just enough of a look to keep them from speaking. Then he said, "All in good time. We know you're a good pilot, so no worries there." He poured another glass for himself and Urgot, then one for Rafe when he lifted it. "In the meantime, let's get to know each other. Rafe says you started learning to pilot under him."

Urgot tried to conceal his annoyance. He took

a drink. Then he launched into telling his background.

After a while, Parn raised the now empty bottle and said, "Man, it's getting late." He put the bottle down and turned to Rafe. "Think we can still catch Mamillo over at Merkellis?"

Rafe said, "Huh? I dunno. Let's try."

"Yeah." Parn stood up and Saicy and Ana did, too. Rafe looked a little puzzled, but then he started to get up, too. Parn said, "Good to meet you, Urgot. We'll get you some more information if we need you."

Parn, Ana, Saicy, and Rafe left the bar. Rafe slugged the half-glasses Ana and Saicy'd left behind. Parn turned them in the direction of Merkellis. Saicy said, "I cross-checked Urgot's conversation against his record. It all matches. He was telling the truth, it seems. There's no evidence that anything was deleted or changed. So that's good, at least."

Ana said, "But what do we really know about him?"

Parn shrugged, then he looked at Rafe. "What do you know about him?"

Rafe looked down at the dusty walkway. "I

dunno. We flew together a few missions when he was training. Seems like a good guy, and definitely a great pilot. But then he got all trained and he went off to fly his own missions. Y'know. I hadn't done more than say hi to him at a bar in a long time."

Ana said, "If he's such a great pilot, why didn't he get picked to fly one of the missions that just got crewed?"

"I'm sure he woulda—he works pretty steady, I guess. But I think he was associate-barred from all the missions that flew recently."

Parn explained to Ana and Saicy about the corporate practice of keeping people from shipping out together to avoid conspiracies.

"Why don't we do that?" Ana asked. "It seems like we're setting ourselves up for a conspiracy."

"Exactly," Parn said. "From corporate's viewpoint, this whole thing is a conspiracy. We're conspiring to take a lot of money out of their pockets."

"Oh," Ana said.

Then they reached Merkellis. Ana paused. She raised a hand, pointing. "Is that . . . ?"

"It's a brothel."

"And that?" She pointed at the conversion

board, with its compatibility ratings for all the different species and their respective genders.

Parn briefly explained the codes. He gestured for her to enter, but she hesitated. He went first, and she followed close behind, her hand on his shoulder.

On a planet like Xythas, colonized largely by two species, it was easy to forget the incredible diversity of the Commonwealth. You saw a few different species in the port: a startling body plan or two scattered in among the majority species. But when you entered the brothel, you saw a hundred species or more. It always took Parn aback. Bipeds, tripeds, quadrupeds, and creatures without any legs at all. There were arms, tentacles, wings, and vestigial limbs of all kinds. Creatures lounged or walked in all states of dress and undress, with elaborate clothes or showing skin, fur, scales, feathers, exoskeletons, and other surfaces. There was even a sentient colloid that oozed by. The possibilities were vertiginous.

That is what Merkellis strove to offer. It wanted to put the entire diversity of the galaxy at the tip of your dick or whatever appendage it was your pleasure to use. Not all the species in the Commonwealth were represented at Merkellis, Parn was pretty sure. But it wasn't for lack of trying.

And with that diversity, there were problems with compatibility. That was the main issue Mamillo dealt with. Parn remembered him talking one time they were traveling together. Parn thought he mostly helped workers who were victims of violence. Mamillo said, "Violence is a problem, but the bigger concern is people pushing themselves to take things their body just wasn't meant for."

"But the compatibility board . . ."

"Yeah, that's posted, but it's just a guideline. Some patrons come in specifically looking to break somebody. And the workers, well, they work hard. They're trying to earn a living, and sometimes . . . well, the money looks bigger. Until it goes in. And then it's a problem."

"You ever have to separate people surgically?"

"Yeah. More times than I'd like to remember. But it's worse when they separate themselves. Serious trauma."

Parn was thinking of this memory when he spotted Mamillo sitting on the far side of the lounge. It wasn't hard to find alien species that looked more human than Mamillo. He was very tall and very slender. His face bore the marks of many fights. He never started them, but he couldn't keep out of them. He put his face in front of dozens of punches, a few blades, and at least one bullet and one flame. Surgeons put his face back together reasonably well, but he'd never sprung for the cosmetic surgery that would make him look human again. And his skin had a distinctly greyish cast.

If you had to guess, you probably couldn't have named the species he belonged to. You certainly wouldn't guess human first. And you'd almost be right. He was tank grown. Two mothers and a father. Three different planets. It was a whim of passion, and the passion had burned out by the time he was decanted. None of them had wanted to raise him. He'd been in alien orphanages all his life, so he felt comfortable with the mix of species at Merkellis. Much more than with an all-human crew.

When Parn asked him why he shipped out then, Mamillo said, "The money's good," just like every corer and coolie. But unlike the corers and coolies, you never saw Mamillo living the high life when he got back. He just settled back in at the brothel, where, Parn suspected, he wasn't paid for his work. If anything, he paid for the privilege. There was always scuttlebutt that he'd bought a ticket home for one hard luck case or another.

"Mamillo," Parn called out. He strode across the room and, unthinking, offered his hand. It only took a moment for Parn to recall his mistake, and he let his hand fall to his side. Mamillo's right hand was badly burned when he tried to deflect an acid attack. It had taken a long time for him to learn how to practice left-handed. "Mamillo, I'm here because I'm hoping you'll join our crew."

"Yep," Mamillo said. "I expected that."

"You can't be serious. How'd you expect us to come in with this offer?"

Mamillo gestured absently with his left hand. "This place is like a bilge. All the rumors eventually collect here. And the latest ones about you say you've stolen a map to an alleged pepper planet."

Now Parn was scratching the back of his head. "Well, yeah, I've got a map. But I didn't steal it."

Mamillo leaned back in his seat. "That's not what Astreyan says. He also says that he's going to kill you and anyone who tries to ship out with you."

"Ha! I'm not afraid of him. And you're not, either, are you? Well, what do you think about shipping out with us?"

"Well . . ." Mamillo paused. His jaw moved side to side. "I've had worse offers, I think. What's the pay?"

"That depends. Do you want an up-front rate or do you want shares?"

Mamillo moved his jaw from side to side again. "I think I want shares."

"Great, then you negotiate with me!"

In fifteen minutes, they'd worked out a deal that everyone was happy with. Saicy called up revised contracts, and Ana, Parn, and Mamillo signed. Mamillo even had a recommendation for an engineer named Birque. Parn felt everything was going more smoothly than he'd thought possible, but that changed when they left the bordello.

Astreyan waited outside in the dusty street. He was flanked by several men who looked like cops at first. A closer look at their uniforms, though, showed them to be private security troops. Hired guns. Astreyan wasn't wearing a uniform: he wore clothes similar to the ones Parn had received from Saicy, but his shirt was viridian, and his pants were a deeper green.

Astreyan shook his head. "I had hoped you were here to return my map. But I guess the rumors are true: you're trying to turn that stolen map into stolen pepper. This is your last chance to give it over."

Parn said, "It's not stolen. Vigar gave it to me. Passing it down like father to son, he said."

Astreyan laughed. "Now that's a good one! I hadn't heard that one before. Thanks for the joke. What makes that so funny is, see, I'm his son. That map should be mine!"

Parn reeled. Ana steadied him. Vigar had never mentioned that Astreyan was his son. Vigar told him that his son was dead. Parn remembered seeing Astreyan get up angrily from Vigar's table once. He asked Vigar about it, but the old corer hadn't wanted to talk. Shortly after that he'd decided to give the map to Parn. Parn never made the connection, and even now he was having a hard time understanding it. Why would Vigar lie to him like that?

Astreyan continued, his hand making a fist.

"That map has been in my family for nearly a thousand years. Parent to child, it's been passed down. Until my father, who didn't give it to me, but to a stranger. That map is mine. First you stole my father's love, and then you stole the map."

Parn's voice quivered. "I—I didn't know . . ."

As Parn's voice trailed off, Ana said, "Can you prove it?"

But before Astreyan could answer, Saicy stepped forward. "It doesn't matter."

Astreyan looked at Saicy. "So, you're his investor? I think I know you. You're that cheap screamer Saicy Marin."

"Maris, and I get paid very well for my screams, thank you."

"Are you prepared to become an accessory to his crime? You know how the authorities are when it comes to pepper crimes."

Saicy waved dismissively. "I've established the provenance of the map thoroughly." She tossed her head, and her hair caught the wind briefly then fluttered down. It was at this point that Parn noticed the tiny drones hovering around, presumably filming everything. Saicy stepped forward dramatically, now standing between Parn and Astreyan.

"The law doesn't say a father has to give anything to his son. The transfer deed is fully in order. It shows the transfer from Vigar Tlaloc to Parnassus Jackson. Identities confirmed to UMC specs. Legally binding."

Astreyan pointed at Parn. "My father was deceived by this con-man. He made a mistake."

"Nevertheless, the cortex patterns establish that he was healthy in mind and fully capable of making legally binding decisions. The map belongs to Mr. Jackson."

"I don't care," Astreyan said. "It should be mine and I will have it!" Astreyan made a motion, and his security troops drew their guns.

The robots immediately moved in front of Saicy. Their blindingly pink arms split open to reveal many different types of weapons, all painted pink.

"Automatic threat recognition is a useful feature of these security robots. Keep this up, Astreyan, and I'll get to demonstrate more of the outstanding benefits that make these Xantseco personal protection robots such a great value."

Mamillo was slower than the robots, but now

he put himself between the two groups. "I won't let you people spill blood right here in the street."

Saicy threw back her head and laughed. "Aren't you adorable!" She blew Mamillo a kiss. "But don't worry, doctor, I can demonstrate some of the more advanced Xantseco features like No Harm Disarm!"

As soon as she spoke these words, the robots pounced. They jumped into the air over Mamillo and landed right in front of the security troops. The troops called out in surprise and pain as the robots took away their guns. Some of the guards got shots off, but these deflected off the robots' armor.

Astreyan looked around helplessly at his security guards rolling on the ground. One of them was cradling his hand. "You call that 'No harm'?" he whimpered.

Mamillo was just as stunned but when the guard called out, he sprang to the man's side. After a brief exam he said, "Yeah, I bet that hurts, but there's no lasting harm."

Saicy looked at a drone and winked. "See, it works just as advertised." Then, to Mamillo,

"Would you like to record a medical testimonial? It'd be worth your while."

He frowned back at her. "I don't think I'd feel comfortable endorsing these battle robots."

"Personal protection robots. But it's okay, you can take your time." Then she looked at Astreyan. "They can also apprehend dangerous individuals and turn them over to the authorities."

Astreyan tried not to flinch. He almost succeeded. "This isn't over," he said.

"No, I'm afraid it is. You've lost legally, and illegally—so there!"

Astreyan didn't reply. He headed off at a fast walking pace. His security guards had gotten up and trotted after him, but he pretended not to know them.

"Thank you," Ana said to Saicy. "That could've ended badly!"

Saicy turned on Ana and Parn. She was smiling broadly. She put one hand on Ana's shoulder and one on Parn's. "Thank you! This is great! The ratings on my personal channel are spiking! They'd been flagging for a while and I was trying to figure out my next plot arc. I was thinking about a new boyfriend, engagement, pregnancy, miscarriage—but I'd hashed through all those plots be-fore. I thought about marrying a guy who already had kids so I could jump straight to teen comedy. But, ugh, did I really want to deal with that?

"This, though," she gestured at the robots that were scanning and disabling the weapons they'd taken, "is ratings gold. And I'll probably be able to keep my contract with Xantseco, now. That alone makes this investment profitable."

CHAPTER 12

Saicy and Ana worked together to assemble most of the details for the voyage, such as a ship and provisions, while Parn continued to work on the crew problem. In the second interview, Urgot, the pilot Rafe recommended, looked aggressively at Parn as they talked. They went over his experience, working with Rafe, and his aspirations as a pilot. After half an hour of talking to him, Parn wasn't sure.

He pulled off and talked to Saicy and Ana. "I dunno about this guy. I'm not sure we can trust him."

"I'm not sure we have a choice," Saicy said. "I was dubious about your method, so I've been soliciting licensed pilots through the job boards. Not a lot of response. And those who start out interested drop out once they find out what the expedition is. It seems that Astreyan has poisoned the well and made many people reluctant to work with us."

Parn frowned. "Maybe we should make Astreyan an offer. He might deserve a share of the expedition." He couldn't help thinking that Vigar's blood son had some right to expect something from his family legacy.

Ana said, "No! Whatever right he had to shares he gave up when he decided to come after us. He deserves nothing."

Parn didn't say anything. He didn't look at either of his partners. Saicy waved dismissively. "Your share is yours. You can do what you like with it."

Parn's share had been whittled down in various ways, so all he was really able to offer Astreyan was 10% of the total profits. It was rejected scornfully, "I would be a fool to take 10% when it should be 100% mine."

When Parn told the women about the response, Saicy was satisfied, but it only made Ana angrier. Saicy redirected the conversation. "We still have to decide on our pilot. I think Urgot might be our only option."

Parn sighed, but he had to agree. They didn't have any other option right now, and with the ship—which Saicy had renamed *Xythan Scream Queen*—waiting in dock, they couldn't spend much more time on the search.

Once they had a legal pilot of record, they could file their flight plan and begin loading the ship with supplies. It took three days before they were ready to depart. For the launch, Ana broke out her tool overalls and gray duster she wore at the rocket club launch. Saicy wore a midi black pencil skirt and tight red sweater. Parn put on his corer uniform, leaving behind the clothes that Ana and Saicy had given him.

Just as they were getting ready to board the shuttle, they heard a call. "Parn, Parn, wait!" Parn stopped and ran down the gangplank. "Mehany!" He called. They embraced at the bottom of the gangplank.

Parn said, "They told me you were already engaged on a voyage."

Mehany smiled. She was also wearing a corer uniform. "I was, but the ship failed inspection at the last minute. All contracts were canceled. As soon as I heard, I began trying to figure out how to reach you. I only just managed to learn where your shuttle was lifting from. I am glad I caught you."

Parn hugged her again. "I'm glad you did." Then he turned to Saicy. "This is Mehany. She's our third corer. Draw up a contract, please."

Saicy gave the orders to her lawyer-bot. It drew up the contract. Mehany skimmed it quickly and agreed. Then they all climbed on board as the shuttle finished its prep for launch. Finally, the engines ignited, and the shuttle lifted off.

In about ten minutes, they docked with the orbital station where *Xythan Scream Queen* was waiting. All their identities and contracts were checked again before they were let on board. Saicy gave them all a tour since she knew the ship better than anyone. The ship didn't smell new, but it was clean. Saicy directed Ana and Parn to the captain's stateroom. It was huge, with a giant, luxuriant bed and more space than would normally be achievable on a voyage like this. But since they were relatively shorthanded, everyone got more space. Even Mehany, who had just signed on, got a room that normally bunked 36 corers sleeping in three shifts. Saicy had fitted it as an extra bedroom.

Saicy ended the tour on the bridge. Urgot took

his place as primary pilot and Rafe took his place as secondary, settling into their custom acceleration couches. They ran through the legal identity checks, then Saicy said, "We have to be prepared. My sources say that Astreyan is planning one more attempt to get control of the map."

Urgot nodded. "If he's going to do it, it'll have to be in the fishing zone."

Parn had heard about the fishing zone, but he didn't know what it was.

Rafe said, "Yeah. There's only a small amount of area where they can actually intercept us. If they try to do it too soon, the cops get on 'em. Wait too long to start shadowing us and they'll never reach us."

Saicy said, "I think that's where they want to hit us. We should start out at best speed and try to keep them from shadowing us too closely before we leave the police zone." She looked at Parn.

Parn felt hot. "I don't know anything about navigation or maneuvers. Ana, do you think that's right?"

"Most actual courses follow that logic." Ana said, "We never plot them that way, but that's how they come back to us."

Parn nodded. "Let's do that, then. "

Saicy gestured for Parn to sit down in the captain's chair. He hesitated until Ana encouraged him. "We made up our minds. You have to be captain."

"Me? Why?"

Ana gripped his hand. "Your map, and you brought us all together."

Saicy said with a smile, "That, and you don't have a job on the ship."

Parn chuckled. He sat down in the chair and was surprised at how well it fit his form.

"Fits great, huh?" Saicy said, smiling. She gestured at the navigator's station. "Ana scanned you secretly so we could keep this a surprise."

Parn turned to Ana. "Thanks. Yes, it is a huge surprise." Then he turned to the pilot's station. "Okay. Urgot, let's fire up the engines and get going."

"Not the worst command I've been given." Urgot turned back to the control panel. "Docking clamps disengaged. And . . . we're underway."

The thrust pulled everyone down to the floor as the engines ramped up slowly, both to keep from throwing anyone to the ground and to clear the dock. Everyone cheered. Then things got quiet on the deck. Urgot monitored the computers. Rafe sat back in his chair and chewed something that smelled like licorice.

Parn was getting a little bored. He stood up. Walked around. Sat down in the captain's chair. He was able to call up all the consoles. He could also get feeds from all the cameras in the ship. He scrolled through all the empty corridors. Mehany, Seldon, Birque, and Mamillo were not on the bridge. She was in her cabin with the privacy setting on. He could override that, he thought, but he wasn't sure if that was true or just corer scuttlebutt. Seldon was relaxing in the crew lounge. Birque was in engineering. Parn didn't know where Mamillo was.

Parn called up Ana's panels, and found out he didn't understand anything on her screens. Saicy didn't call up any screens from her seat. Instead, she spoke to her assistant, Cap, a small robot whose oblong body was about 20 cm by 30 by 10. It had extended its four spindly legs so it could get close to her lips. It looked vaguely like a gibbon doing a crabwalk. She whispered a steady stream of words to it. Parn couldn't hear them, only got the sense of the sibilant sounds and the movement of her lips.

Parn sighed. Time stretched on.

"We've got something," Urgot said suddenly. "It's a ship, and it's loosely paralleling us. The computer thinks there's a 75% chance the course similarity is nonaccidental."

Parn said, "So that's Astreyan or his men?"

"Maybe. A couple more course corrections should tell." Although the overall acceleration of the ship had now reached nearly three g's, the course corrections were just tiny nudges. "Yep, now the computer is saying that it's 98% likely the course similarity is nonaccidental. Traffic control has picked it up, too. They're flagging our courses."

Parn got a message on his console. He couldn't understand all the legal language, but he could parse out that it was, essentially, asking him if he wanted to dock with the other vessel. He sent a negative reply. Traffic control recommended course changes. When the other ship mirrored their course changes, both ships received copies of the order to "obtain discrete courses." Urgot tried to obey. The other ship defied the order.

Saicy said, "Now's the time to start evasive maneuvers."

"Yep," Urgot said. He looked at Parn.

"Uh, lemme sound the warning, then go ahead." Parn hit the high g warning, which gave everyone thirty seconds to get to a safe place. That should be enough most anywhere in the ship. He strapped into his couch, which was designed to absorb the stress of maneuvers and, if necessary, impacts. They could soften the abrupt jerk of 15 or 20 gs/second down to something a little more manageable like two or three. Prolonged acceleration would still be a problem, but these would make them safe for maneuvering.

Once the thirty seconds had expired, Urgot said, "Let's see what they can do."

There was an intense period of changing force from all different directions. Even with the inertial couches, it was brutal. Parn felt sore all over, as if he had one big bruise from head to foot.

At the end of it, Urgot sighed. "Well, I think I've pushed them to their limit—and ours. We can't outrun them, but they won't be able to match course and speed for boarding."

Parn gave a sigh of relief. "Can I unstrap, then?"

"No, they're not giving up, yet. We're going to have to keep maneuvering, but the numbers don't lie. They won't board us."

Urgot wasn't lying about the maneuvers. They went on as before. Then he announced, "They're giving up now. They've stopped trying to match course and speed, but they'll still pass too close for comfort." After a short pause, he said, "Dammit! They've passed us a high-density data package. It's unfolding itself. Yep, yep, it's a suite of viruses."

Saicy said, "The ship's countermeasures are all up to industry standards. They won't crack."

"Let's hope you're right," Urgot said.

Rafe said, "Looks like it. Navigation virus defeated. Life support virus defeated. Reactor control defeated. A few others, too. But it looks like there's one here the ship can't ID."

"Send it to my assistant. She'll know what it is." At the mention, Cap lifted herself up on her spindly legs and crawled over to a data port. Rafe sent the information.

Saicy's assistant spoke in a bright, chirpy voice not unlike Saicy's. "This virus is designed to attack the Xantseco Personal Protection Robots. It seems likely that they have been compromised."

This news caused a heavy silence to fall in the room. It was broken by the sound of metal contacting metal. The security robots were on the move, and they were frighteningly close.

"Shit," Rafe said, looking around. "This place is a fucking dead end. I gotta get outta here before they cut me off!"

"Wait!" Saicy said, but it was too late. He was up and out of his seat. The door was open, and he was out the room faster than Parn would've expected given the two gs acceleration.

But he didn't make it far. There was a short burst of gunfire and blood splattered into the bridge through the still-closing door. The ferrous smell of blood mixed with nitrogen-based propellant filled the bridge. Ana gasped. Blood patterned the floor mere centimeters from her feet. She unstrapped immediately and moved toward the main console at the front of the bridge.

Saicy spoke to her assistant, "Cut off their door clearance, Cap."

"Yes, Mistress."

The robots walked up to the security door. They paused, waiting for it to open. Then there was another burst of gunfire. The door seemed un-affected.

"So, that's it? The door keeps them out and we stay in here?" Urgot said.

Saicy shook her head. "The robots are designed to be usable on ships like this. Their guns *shouldn't* pierce the bulkheads or door. But they have other strengths."

To emphasize her point, the door bulged slightly.

"Shit!" Urgot said.

Parn had unstrapped himself and was looking around for any kind of improvised weapon.

"But," Saicy said, "it's not as bad as all that. The bridge has another exit. Let's go."

The exit turned out to be a small hole under the main control panel. Saicy's assistant went first, then Saicy waved Ana through. Ana crawled in.

"Oh, and make sure you lock the main controls," Saicy called back at Urgot.

"Already done," Urgot said. He started getting ready to follow Saicy through, but Parn pushed past so he had to follow up in the rear.

Then Parn realized that they hadn't warned Mehany and Mamillo. He got on his com and called Mehany. "Mehany, Mehany," he called when the channel came open, "some of Saicy's robots got hacked. They're going crazy. Watch out!"

"No shit," Mehany said. "we've got one here. Mamillo's got a plan. He thinks it will work. But it involves using me as bait." Gunfire. "Suck on a sump!" Mehany yelled. "Okay, I'm gonna need to call you back." She closed the channel.

"Can we get going now?" Urgot asked, gesturing forward. There was little room in the tunnel, and certainly not enough for him to climb past Parn.

Parn nodded and crawled after Saicy, whose outfit was obviously not designed for crawling. It stretched tight across her buttocks and rode up her thighs as she crawled. The view was also making it hard for Parn to crawl.

Behind them, they heard the door giving way. The robots strode into the bridge. Parn looked back, but they had left the bridge behind around several turns.

"They're not coming after us, are they?" Urgot asked.

"No," Saicy said. "They won't fit."

"Is that by design?" Ana asked.

"Yeah, sort of," Saicy replied. "This escape tunnel is part of the reason why we picked this ship design. And the fact that the robots couldn't fit was a definite plus, although Cap considered their hacking to be a very low order risk."

"My apologies, mistress," the robot chirped.

"Yeah, the tunnel's great and all," Urgot said, "but where's it taking us?"

"It'll open up into the hold. If we need to make a stand, that's the best place to do it. Although hopefully Cap will have regained control by then. Progress?"

"It's going slowly. The factory-installed safeguards have been overridden. The new safeguards are more . . . robust." The tone in the assistant's voice made it seem that it didn't like to disappoint its mistress.

Parn didn't know whether robots could really feel or not. He knew that robot experiences had been legally defined as "not feelings" but this would not be the first time in Parn's experience where legal definitions did not match reality. He also knew that for taxation purposes, star pepper was not legally in the category of luxury goods. Except for the harvesting spiders, he hadn't ever spent much time with robots. He knew the spiders all seemed to be a little different, but he'd been reluctant to describe that as having "personality." That would make disabling and discarding the robots at the end of a harvesting expedition tantamount to mass murder.

They crawled on through the escape tunnel, taking several more turns before descending a ladder and resuming their horizontal crawl. They did this several times. Then they reached a hatch. Ana hesitated for a moment.

Saicy said, "Cap, open the hatch." The robot, its legs now condensed to fit the tunnel, crawled past Ana and worked on the hatch. It opened with a gentle chuff. Ana moved from a crawl to a crouch, took two steps forward, then stood up. The assistant followed her out. Saicy crawled out next. She stood up with a groan, pushed her skirt down, then stretched.

Parn came out next, and he looked around the room. It was a large hold, and essentially empty, except for a small cluster of boxes near the hatch where they emerged. The space that they wanted for star pepper completely dwarfed their need for supplies.

Urgot came out last, looked around, and sighed.

"Smut," Saicy said, even as Urgot said, "So, what do we do now?"

Saicy shook her head. "I thought this would lead us to the hold where my mecha was. They were supposed to put it here. But, apparently, they left these supplies here and the mecha is in the next hold."

"No problem," Ana said, breaking into a jog, "we can get to the next hold across this way." Parn could see the hatch she was headed for. He had a vague memory of going through the hatch when they'd toured the ship earlier. Parn nodded, but he didn't start to move.

Then he heard the sound of a different door opening. He turned his head to look, as did everyone else. "Smut," Urgot said, and Parn thought that summed it up. One of the protection bots stood in the open doorway. It scanned the area and paused momentarily to pick its targets.

Saicy shot her assistant a withering glance, and spat, "Door privileges."

Cap shrank down on its compressable legs. "I am sorry, mistress, this is a different security protocol. I did not think it would be necessary, so I deprioritized it to put maximum resources toward regaining control."

Parn yelled, "Ana, look out!" But she had her own plans. She broke into a full run, even as the robot released a burst of shots toward the small group of people near the escape tunnel.

Saicy's assistant was hit, and Saicy screamed, "Capella!" Then she cried out incoherently and fell as red chunky splatters came off her. There were some metallic impacts and dull thuds, too, as bullets struck around the area. Parn saw that it would be too slow for them to get into the tunnel. Instead, he grabbed Saicy by the shoulder and dragged her behind a cargo container. Parn heard a second burst of bullets firing and rebounding off some metal and plastic in the direction of the far hatch. As he pulled Saicy, he tried to see in the direction of the hatch. He got a brief glance. There didn't seem to be any blood. Based on the bloody trail that Saicy was leaving behind, there probably would be if Ana'd been hit.

As he got Saicy behind the crates, he had to duck down because a third burst of gunfire struck around them. The gunfire just bounced off the bulkhead and the crate.

Saicy sucked air through her teeth. "Well, at least the ammunition works as advertised. It's not piercing the hull, but it sure was hell on my arm. I think the bone's completely shattered. It hurts like hell. And look at all the blood!" Parn was trying not to look at the blood, which was pooling around her on the ground in alarming quantities. Saicy's head sagged.

Ana's voice came over the com, "I'm here! What should I do?"

Saicy perked up, though her face was still alarmingly pale. "You can't do anything unless I authorize you. I need my assistant for that."

Parn glanced around the corner. The assistant was still where it had fallen. It was almost within reach, twitching and sparking in a pool of its own blood, which was spreading alongside Saicy's, grey and immiscible. Its components were scattered in an arc behind it.

The security robot sprayed the crate with gunfire just as Parn ducked back behind. The robot had a good response time, but what he really needed was to catch it anticipating. He raised his hand up three times in a regular count. Then, before he would have raised it a fourth time, he broke from cover and grabbed the assistant. Sure enough, the robot anticipated where his hand would be, sending a burst of bullets at the empty air and giving Parn just enough time to grab one of the assistant's long legs. The robot shot at him again, and it was almost too late—he'd already gotten the assistant back. It slid along the bloody ground and ran into Saicy. But he hadn't gotten his left hand fully back into cover, and a bullet struck his ring finger, exploding it into tiny fragments.

Parn yelled and shook his hand once. Then he pressed his right hand onto the stump of his finger, trying to stop the blood that was pouring out.

Saicy had drifted again, but the sound seemed to startle her back to awareness. "Okay," she said when she saw the assistant in front of her. She went to reach for it with her right arm, but only a little bit of the upper arm moved. The rest of her arm just sagged there, bending right in the middle of what should have been her humerus. She looked at it briefly, then sagged back against the crate.

Parn looked to Urgot for help. He wasn't exactly panicked, but he wasn't doing anything. He seemed resigned to the situation. He leaned back against the bulkhead and looked at Parn. Parn sighed, then pulled himself forward. He sat up next to Saicy. He took his shirt off and wrapped it around Saicy's arm. He tried to apply pressure, but the arm was squishy and pressure made her hurt. She came to alertness again, and looked at Parn first, then started casting around for her assistant. When she saw it, she gave Parn a wan smile. "You know why I only trust robots?"

Urgot snorted. "You trust robots, huh? How's that working out for you?"

Saicy looked at him. Her effort to smile was shown by just a slight quiver in her cheek muscles. "Admittedly, not great in this case. But there's one good reason why I trust them: you can fix them if they're broken." She moved her left hand in a subtle pattern on her thigh and a small pocket appeared. She reached in and pulled out some small tools and a thin grey case. She opened the little broken robot easily. Then she made a grunt. "I can fix this, but it's going to take time. Can you get me more time?"

Parn snuck a quick glance around the crate. The robot was getting close. He didn't know how much time Saicy needed, but the robot would be here soon. He looked around for any resource he could use. Then his eyes lighted on the fire suppression panel behind Urgot.

He gestured. "Open that up and pull out the grenades."

"Huh?" Urgot said.

"Behind you," Parn gestured.

Urgot turned and opened the panel. He pulled out a bandolier and handed it to Parn. "Take the other one," Parn said.

Urgot hesitated.

"Do it. This isn't much, but it should be enough to keep that thing busy until she's ready."

Urgot pulled out the second bandolier. "Why don't we just trigger the fire suppression system?" He gestured to the lever.

"Flooding the room with foam would make it impossible to breathe, and I think Saicy works faster with oxygen."

"Yes, thank you," Saicy chimed in. "I'm like fire that way."

Parn thought Saicy was like fire in many ways. He peeked around the crate again. Then he quickly threw the first grenade. He'd meant to hit the head, but it landed at the robot's feet. It exploded, releasing a sphere of foam a meter across. Although it didn't hit where he intended, it helped nonetheless. The robot began to slip and had to move more slowly, carefully picking its steps across the cargo bay.

Parn sighed and pulled off another grenade. He barely managed to chuck it before the robot shot at him. But this time, the grenade struck true. The foam burst around the robot's head. Parn knew that the cold, opaque foam would blind the robot briefly. But how long, he didn't know.

"Let's take her." He gestured for Urgot to grab Saicy's other arm. They pulled her over to a position behind another row of crates. And then Parn saw the forklift loader. After they had Saicy supported against a crate, Parn tapped Urgot on the shoulder. "Go keep it distracted. I'm gonna try something."

Urgot shook his head and clearly wanted to say "No." But he actually said, "Okay, I'll try."

Parn hit his shoulder hard now. "Superb! Give it hell."

Urgot moved nervously back to the crates where they had first taken shelter. Parn watched as he hesitantly peered over the top of the crates. The security robot had managed to clear away the foam and it quickly got a bead on Urgot. A burst of bullets rebounded off the crate as Urgot ducked down. He looked at Parn, his eyes pleading for relief. Parn gestured encouragingly.

Then Parn was startled by a loud smack right beside him. His head snapped around and looked at Saicy. A pale pink handprint was fading on the skin of her cheek, which was chalky white. She didn't look up, but she said, "Sorry. I'm just trying to stay awake." She was messing around with the tiny circuitry in her assistant.

Parn then heard another grenade going off. He looked back over his shoulder and saw that Urgot had encased the head of the robot in foam. He made a run for the loader.

He had often driven this type of loader on harvesting trips. He quickly got it detached from the wall. He rotated it around to face toward the robot as he raised the lift plate to protect his face. As the plate blocked his view, a safety camera came on to show him his blind spot.

The robot fired at the loader, but the bullets bounced off the lift plate. Using the blind spot camera, Parn navigated to face the robot. The blind spot camera wasn't designed to be the sole forward viewer, but it was enough for Parn to get around the crates and face directly at the robot over an open straightaway. As he came around the crate near Saicy, he heard her say, "Don't worry about that sound, that's just the camera drones launching. You focus on the powerup status. When it's all green, you're ready to go."

Then Parn hit the accelerator for the loader, charging directly at the robot. The loader was low and heavy with magnetic wheels for stability in microgravity, so it wasn't fast under the best of conditions. But under two g's acceleration from the main engines, the loader seemed to crawl at first, although it picked up speed gradually.

The robot fired several bursts at the lift plate, but when it realized it couldn't penetrate, it seemed to wait for the loader, then dodged out of the way at the last second. But it didn't know the loader had been designed to maneuver in the tightest of spaces. Parn took advantage of the ability and got it turned around to face the robot. Almost.

The loader tumbled sideways. Parn was thrown clear as the loader crushed over the robot. After his grunts of pain, Parn said, "Yeah!" Then he tried to stand and tumbled back to the ground. His ankle hurt and didn't want to support his weight.

Then the loader tilted. The robot was damaged, but not destroyed. Parn began to scoot away as the robot tipped the loader off itself. He managed to scoot behind a crate before the robot managed to target him.

Parn wasn't behind the same crate as Saicy, but he could see her from where he was. She wasn't working on her assistant anymore. She was just leaning back against the crate with half-lidded eyes. For a moment, Parn thought she was dead, but then she blinked.

The robot was dragging itself closer to where they were hiding. Step. Scrape. Step. Scrape. It came around the crate, obviously worse for the wear. The targeting was slow as it raised its gun to shoot Parn, who felt he had nothing left to run with.

Then there was a tremendous sound of tearing and buckling metal. The robot turned to face the source of the sound. It raised its gun to target the new threat, but a missile whooshed into it, blowing it to pieces.

Parn lifted himself up to look over the crate. There was Ana, in Saicy's pink mecha. She waved. Parn, Urgot, and Saicy all cheered. Then Saicy fell back, hit the crate, and slunk limp to the floor.

"Shit!" Parn yelled and began scooting toward her. That's when he heard the strange beeping sound. He activated his com. "Mamillo, Saicy's dying here, you've got to come get her."

"I can't," Mamillo said. "There are two robots here and we can just barely keep them down. Get her here and I can take care of her."

"Send Mehany, then!"

"I can't. There are two robots. Both of us are keeping them down. You need to get her here!"

"Where's Seldon?" There was no response.

Parn waved to Ana. Then he scooted over to Saicy's side. "What is that beeping? Is that a vital sign readout from the mecha?"

"No," Ana said as the mecha drew close, "there's nothing coming from here. Where's it coming from?"

Parn grunted, then said to Ana, "Gently move that crate out of the way and pick her up."

Ana nodded. She pivoted to face Saicy. The arm of the mecha moved, hitting the crate, which flew across the cargo bay. When it struck the wall, it burst open, sending food packets spraying everywhere.

"Uh, I don't think I can do anything gently."

Parn looked at Saicy, her face grown pale and her energy spent. He didn't know how long she might have to live. He put one of his feet under him. He gently tested his ankle. If he didn't flex it, it would hold, although it hurt like hell. His bloody hand on her bloody arm, he picked up Saicy across his shoulders. Despite her weakness, she held on to her assistant. Parn set off at best speed, carefully avoiding bending his ankle.

It was in the elevator that the beeping really got to Parn. It sounded so loud and persistent that he almost wanted to drop Saicy on the ground and seek out the source. But he managed to hold onto his sanity. Then the elevator stopped and Parn walked out. He hurried to the infirmary. Inside, he laid Saicy on a surgical bed.

He wanted to just collapse then, but Mamillo gestured that he had to take over dosing the robot with strong charges from the defibrillators that kept it disabled.

Parn grunted. "Mamillo, goddammit, if you do anything, can you please stop that beeping?"

"I can't," he said, and gestured to Saicy's assistant. After dosing his robot, Parn took the two steps over to look at it.

Saicy had posted the video of Ana in the mecha. The beeping was notifications of all the likes, comments, and repostings rolling in.

CHAPTER 13

The video turned out to be Saicy's most popular ever. Billions of people on Xythas watched it, and when it went out via hyperpulse to the rest of the Commonwealth, it was seen by trillions of beings. As she convalesced, she had a lot of time to focus on the numbers. It helped keep her spirits up as she healed. For someone whose primary experience with serious injury was the videostories she acted in, the actual process of healing was (literally) painfully slow.

"I thought modern medicine was fast," she confided to Parn on one of his daily visits.

"It is," Parn said. "I think. Someone with your injuries probably would've been dead before. Or would've spent several pentads recovering. Even I would've taken time to recover, and I would still be missing a finger."

She frowned.

Another day, she told Parn that the revenue from that video alone had paid for her investment in the voyage. The mecha company had renewed her contract—at double the compensation—and scheduled a new series of ads based on the fight in the cargo hold. And although the defense robot company had canceled her contract, the settlement on the personal injury lawsuit she filed would likely be worth double the revenue from those ads. Then she told Parn that the next day he should bring Ana with him—there was an opportunity for her.

"I don't want to see her," Ana said. "It's bad enough that you have to see her every day—I don't see why I should, too."

Parn was sitting on the edge of the bed. The room was sparsely decorated—they hadn't had much time to take care of those things—but Ana had found some images she liked in the onboard library so these displayed on the fixed screens around them, and she'd given the ambient light just the right hint of green she liked. Ana was sitting at the fold-out desk, working on navigation figures related to their jump through Rho Space. The original figures were invalidated by the evasive maneuvers Urgot had been forced to take and the unguided acceleration while they were under attack from the robots.

Parn said, "I'm the captain. She's a member of our crew. She's wounded. Shouldn't I visit her? If Rafe were alive, I'd be visiting him every day."

"Yeah, I suppose so. But that doesn't mean I have to."

Parn stood up and walked over to her. "No, you don't have to. But she said it was an opportunity for you."

Ana clenched her fingers into half-closed fists. Then she gestured broadly around the room as she turned to Parn. "This is an opportunity! This expedition. Isn't that enough?"

"Sure." Parn shrugged. "But there's not much to do now. Maybe this can help fill the time."

"For you, maybe, your job doesn't really start until we get to the planet. But for me, this is my busiest time."

"Yeah, maybe so. But maybe it will be good to do something else sometime. And besides, you know there's a chance there won't be any pepper there at all. Or maybe there will be some, but it won't be ripe, and we'll have to sell futures."

Ana sighed. "Fine. I'll go tomorrow. But just this once."

Parn shrugged again. "Sure. After that, you'll know what the opportunity is, and you can decide what you want to do."

When they entered the room, Saicy looked up from the remnants of her assistant, Cap, which she still had hopes of repairing. "Ana!" She smiled and moved the robot parts aside, grabbing her small external display. "Did you see the number of views on my video?"

Ana stopped dead. "Is that why you brought me here? To brag about your video views?" Her hands went to her hips.

Saicy's smile flickered, but didn't go away. "Yes, I mean, not exactly. What I wanted to remind you is that you're one of the stars of the video. And with the hundred trillion eyes that have seen you, you're perfectly positioned to launch your own platform."

"My what?" Her arms fell flat to her side.

"Your platform—uh, your own line of merchandise and advertising. You've got such great exposure now. And, look, I'm getting requests about you."

Ana walked over to the bedside.

Saicy tilted the screen. "This is the list of requests. You can scroll down if you want, but most of these are just today. Well, that's when I got them. With the hyperpulse schedule, some of the distant ones may be a few days old."

Ana looked at the list. She scrolled. Then she scowled. "Most of them say, 'Show us your tits!'"

Parn walked over so he could see both women's faces and the screen.

Saicy said, "Well, yes, that's expected. But you can bank on that."

"I'm not going to expose myself for money." Ana's face was getting red. Her tone was angry, accusatory.

"You don't have to, exactly. But some pictures of you in tight or revealing clothes would sell. You could make some good money."

"I'm not comfortable with that. I don't like the thought of what people would be doing with my image."

Saicy laughed. "Well, let me dispel that worry

right now. Look at this." She called up an image of Ana in the mecha cockpit, topless. It was a manipulated image, but it was good, and it looked real. Even the color of her nipples was accurate, and Parn wondered whether that was just a lucky guess or if they had some way of figuring that out.

"What is that?"

"Well, it's you."

"It looks like me, yes. But it's fake."

"Well, it's art. It doesn't pretend to be real, but it's out there. And it's selling. If that's the case, shouldn't you be the one profiting?"

"So you think I should pose for pictures like that and sell them?"

"If you want to—people would flock to a real picture like that. The authenticity is a turn-on, and they'd pay a premium."

Parn saw Ana's fist clenching. It wasn't preparing for a punch. It was clenching hard, driving her nails into her palms as her knuckles went white.

"But you don't have to do any more than you're comfortable with. Even an image as you are now with a little personal message could bring in revenue. And if you wanted to do something in a boudoir-type scenario—that'd sell even better."

Parn looked over Ana's outfit. It was typical of her daily wear. Pants loose on the legs but tight on the buttocks, and a top that was also loose and comfortable, but draped over her breasts and shoulders, outlining their shapes.

"I'm not comfortable selling my body, even if it is just images."

Saicy realized just how angry Ana was getting. She raised a hand in a stop gesture. "Sure, I understand. But what about selling your voice and your brain?"

"Huh?" Ana cocked her head.

"Just record a brief lecture about Rho Space navigating. Your voice, your manner, and your intelligence will make that salable. And if you don't want to develop your own platform, I can sell it with my platform. How's about that?"

Ana sighed. "I don't know if I could do that."

"Sure you can. You're a natural! Just give it a try."

"I'll think about it."

"Great! Now, Parn, there's an opportunity for you, too."

Parn said, "I guess I can do pictures, but I'm certainly not comfortable doing a lecture."

Saicy laughed. "Parn, nobody wants to see your ugly mug! All your heroics were, unfortunately, off camera, so there's not the same demand for your picture. But there is demand for your story. I've been approached with an offer for a fictional version of your story. I'd star, but you've been recast. You'll see a lot of revenue—more than you'd see from pictures, that's for sure!"

Parn grunted. "Okay. That sounds good."

"Wonderful! Just gimme your mark here and I'll get started on it." Parn did. He was vaguely aware of Ana's reaction, but it was too much out of his vision to know what she was feeling.

Saicy turned back to her screen so Parn and Ana took their leave. Outside, Mamillo was directing the growth of his tiny trees. He'd brought them on as seeds, but he was using growth accelerants to direct them into the shapes he wanted. Parn knew about this hobby, but he wasn't sure he'd ever seen the products: fancifully shaped trees in many colors and styles.

Out in the hall, Ana said, "I can't believe you did that!"

"What?" Parn asked. He looked over his shoulder hoping someone else was there.

"Me, she was just asking to sell my image. You, they wanted to buy you, sun, moon, and stars! But what do you do? You just sell your entire identity. And for what? A little money? You hardly looked at the terms!"

Parn shrugged. "It's not like that at all. They wanted my story. What's that to me? It's my past. If I can make money off what I've already done—that's got to be the easiest money I'll ever make."

"But, don't you see? They're recasting you. In the mind of everyone who sees those stories—trillions of people—you won't be you, you'll be him. And he'll be whatever Saicy wants him to be."

"But I don't see why that matters. What are those people to me?"

Ana clenched her fingers in the air as if she wanted to grab the idea and smash it over Parn's head. Her voice was slow and low, but acid. "You won't be making an image for yourself, you'll be making it for someone else! You won't be making a legacy for yourself, you'll be making it for someone else! And Saicy, she'll just attach it onto her own. She'll own the part of you that's out there, the part that lasts."

"What are you talking about? I'd be making the money. What else matters?" But when he mentioned money again, something clicked in his brain. He had a sense that these words Ana was using: "image" and "legacy" were to himself something like what "credit" was to real money. It was a kind of currency that allowed Saicy to live in the world she lived in. It allowed Ana to move in and out of doors that were barred to him, that made bankers see him as a bad risk. And he began to think that, maybe, he really had given away something of real value for something that wasn't as valuable as it seemed.

He was working out how to articulate this insight when Ana huffed and shook her head. Then she turned away, her hands moving as if she were in silent conversation with an invisible man. Perhaps the image of Parn.

Parn stood in the hall by himself for a while. Then he turned the opposite direction and walked. He hadn't thought where he was going, so of course he found himself in a dead-end corridor. Ana'd walked toward the elevators. Retracing his steps that far seemed like defeat for Parn, who was still reeling from the revelation that Saicy might have swindled him. So he only walked halfway back to the ladder. When he got there, he looked at the rungs running up toward his room. They seemed so high and the effort to climb them in 2 g's seemed so great. He sighed and went down a couple levels to the bunk room that had been converted into a rec room.

Mehany and Urgot were playing tabletop hockey. Seldon was sitting on the far side of the table, watching. During the robot battle, he had been in his cabin, and the robots hadn't had time to get to him. Parn came up and stood beside the table. Mehany smacked the puck across the blue frictionless plastic rink with the expected strength but surprising subtlety. It swept past Urgot's defense for a score.

Mehany cheered, "That's another game for me!"

Urgot just groaned.

Parn said, "You guys been playing long?"

Urgot said, "That's our eleventh game today."

Mehany chortled, "And I'm beating him seven to four."

Urgot quickly added, "But I'm winning the series three days to one."

"Yeah, but if I win this, my margin today will wipe out all those one-point games."

Urgot sighed as he hit the puck. "I told you that's not how we're scoring it. Each day is a best of fifteen, but at the end of the day, it only counts as one win or one loss. The margin doesn't matter."

Mehany made two quick hits, one driving the puck back toward her own corner, the second sending it curving toward Urgot's goal. It almost slipped back behind his paddle, but he deflected it back. "Is that what we agreed to?" Mehany said as she hit the puck hard and straight. Urgot moved his paddle, anticipating another curve, and the puck slid into the goal.

"Shit," Urgot said.

After a few points, won 2–1 by Mehany, Parn said to Urgot, "Aren't you supposed to be on the bridge?"

Urgot shook his head. "Nu-uh. I can't make any changes to the course until Ana tells me what they are."

"Okay," Parn said. He knew that it would still be more than a pentad before they would be fast enough to enter Rho Space. That's when the course needed to be perfect. So he didn't push Urgot. Instead, Parn watched the rest of the games, and he cheered when Mehany won the day. Then he said to Urgot, "You should probably go check in on the bridge."

"Yeah, sure," Urgot replied. He put the paddle down hard. He left. Seldon didn't say anything but ducked out after Urgot.

Mehany walked over to the scoreboard with light, enthusiastic steps. She called up the series score and gave herself one more. Then she turned around, saw Parn looking at her, and sighed. She went over to the water spigot, pulled the water bottle off her belt, and filled it. She took a long drink, then wiped her sweaty brow. She pointed at Parn with the water bottle. "I bet with our crew and the size of this ship, we don't even have to filter the water twice before the end of the trip. That's like fresh water the whole way."

"I like filtered water," Parn said.

"Of course you do. And no greens." She sat down in one of the large, comfortable lounge chairs. Looked away.

Parn kept standing there.

Mehany looked back at him. "You know I don't want to get involved."

"With what?"

"With whatever that look is for. Whatever's going on with you, Ana, and Saicy." She took a drink of water.

"Nothing's going on with us. Nothing really. It's just Ana's mad at me for no reason."

Mehany didn't just roll her eyes: she rolled her entire head. "Oh, believe me. She's got a reason. I've seen enough of my relationships fall apart that I can see the signs a mile away."

"What?" Parn said. He came and sat down next to Mehany, sitting sideways in the seat so he could look at her more easily. He was so close that he could smell her spicy sweat. "I didn't know there was anything wrong. Until she blew up last night. And then this morning. So, tell me what to do."

Mehany looked at Parn "I can't." She sighed, then gestured with her water bottle as she began again, "I mean, I don't know. I've seen it happen so many times. But seeing it doesn't mean I can stop it. No matter what I do, it always crumbles. Just krrrg, right into ruins." She made a motion like a building caving in on itself.

"Well, at least help me know what's wrong—maybe I can figure out what to do."

Mehany laughed. "Good luck. But, sure, tell me what's going on, and I'll see what I can do."

Parn said, "So, anyway, the thing that really made her mad was when I agreed to sell my story to Saicy."

"Stop! That's all I need. It's just like I thought. Ana is jealous of you and Saicy."

"Because of the contract? It doesn't even mean we'll be working together. It's just a story I sold."

"No, look, that's what's set her off, but it's much more than that. I've seen the way you look at Ana: you love her. It's clear. But I've also seen the way you look at Saicy: you worship her. So when you sold her the story, it's like something else you put at her altar. Ana felt slighted."

"Huh," Parn said. He got up and walked across to get himself some water. "Yeah, that tastes pretty good. I dunno what I was thinking."

That evening Parn came back up to his cabin. He hadn't seen Ana the rest of the day. A quick computer inquiry revealed she was taking meals in the cabin. Parn opened the door slowly. Across the room, he saw Ana at her desk, headphones over her ears. The room was dark except for the task light at her desk, and it smelled of half-eaten food.

Parn came up to her, but she was deep in her work. He didn't want to disturb her directly but tried to make himself conspicuous as he bustled around the room, getting ready for bed. He knew she was aware of him when she scowled and pushed her head closer to the screen. When Parn saw that, he threw himself on the bed and lay there, determined to stay awake until she went to bed. But it didn't take long for the combination of boredom, warmth, comfort, and exhaustion to put him to sleep.

CHAPTER 14

The next morning, Parn woke up and realized immediately that Ana was in bed, but all was not well. She normally liked to cuddle in sleep, but now she was huddled on her own. She was on the edge of the bed with her back turned to him. He wanted to reach out to her, but the tense back was forbidding, so he got out of bed.

Instead of getting dressed, which could be done quietly, he started clearing away the food dishes from the day before. This created a racket, and he didn't try to do it quietly. As he collected all the food debris and dishes to put them back in the bullet so they could be taken away, he saw Ana had woken up. But when she saw he saw, she closed her eyes and feigned sleep.

Then he made sure he was especially noisy

putting the rest of the dishes away. When the dishes were in the return shaft, he went to his clothes locker. A captain's uniform sat folded beside the heap of coring clothes he had worn the day before. Another set of coring clothes sat folded in the drawer, but he put on yesterday's clothes instead. When the company was running the voyage, they decided what he wore each day. As captain, he would wear what he wanted, and he liked the soft feel of unwashed clothes.

Once he was dressed, he looked over at Ana one more time. Still pretending to be asleep—or maybe she'd fallen back asleep. So he left without saying a word.

As was his habit, he went down to the infirmary. But before he went in to see Saicy, it occurred to him that might not be the best idea. So, instead, he diverted over to where Mamillo was crafting his plants. He started with seeds, and, with generous nutrients and some accelerating growth hormones, caused them to grow into strange shapes. Then he pruned and grafted them together to satisfy some personal vision.

Mamillo didn't look up, but he tilted his head slightly to acknowledge Parn's presence. His eyes were intent on the area where he was coaxing a new green tendril from the gnarled brown stem of a low plant. As he squirted a small amount of liquid from the gun-like dispenser, the tendril stretched out. Once it had grown a little while, a deft movement of Mamillo's opposite hand on the keyboard shifted the hormone balance and the new growth created a knot from which spread three smaller growths. Mamillo shaped two of them into spirals that wrapped around their source branch. The third was grown out, then split again to gain its own spiraling adornments.

Parn looked over the six started plants. Two had green leaves, three blue-green leaves, and one had reddish-brown. He asked, "Are you going to end up with just one plant this trip?"

Mamillo answered without looking up. "I don't know yet. I've never worked with any of these plants before. We'll see where this goes."

Parn watched him work for a while in silence.

Eventually, Mamillo said, "I've seen you come down here every day and stop in to say hi to Saicy, and now you're not. What's wrong?"

Parn looked at Mamillo, who still wasn't looking up from the plants. "I . . . I don't really know.

But something's wrong between Ana and me. And I think Saicy's the cause of it. Maybe. I dunno. Maybe you can help me."

Mamillo sighed. "A lot of people ask me relationship questions, on the ships and at the bordello. I don't know why. If I knew anything about relationships, I probably wouldn't be working with these plants so much, right? But I have seen a lot of relationships, and I think I've figured this out." He paused in his work and raised his scarred face to look at Parn. "Don't shoot someone you love. Don't stab her. Don't even hit her with your hand. Get that down, and the rest of it seems to work itself out, one way or another."

Parn listened. After a short pause, he said, "Okay. But what do I do?"

Mamillo shrugged. "I don't know. Maybe just do something else for a while." Then he went back to the plant, squirting liquid and coaxing the tendrils into the shape he wanted.

Parn sat for a while watching Mamillo. Then he stood up. He left the infirmary. He walked up and down the corridor, thinking. Then he went to the elevator and went back to his cabin.

Ana was inside, working at the terminal. The

cabin smelled of more recently eaten food, reminding Parn that he hadn't eaten breakfast. Ana didn't turn around. Parn came over to the table. He reached out and she flinched. But he wasn't reaching for her. He was reaching for the dishes. "Are you done with these?" he asked.

She gestured noncommittally. Parn took that for a yes, cleaned them up and put them in the return shaft.

Then Parn went over to the bathroom and cleaned his face with a depilatory roller. Once his face was clean and smooth, he put on his captain outfit, putting his corer clothes into a return cannister and dropping them in the shaft. He went down to the cafeteria to eat breakfast. No one was there, so Parn ate in silence, thinking some more. He decided that since Ana's work was the next major hurdle for the expedition, he should try to understand it. He called up information on the cafeteria terminal.

Her part now was plotting the ship's course through Rho Space, a parallel universe. Scientists generally believe that there are an infinite number of parallel universes, although only a few hundred have been discovered. Some argue that there are far fewer than that and claim that many of the universes have been visited repeatedly. The argument is that people have seen so little of each universe that they've described different parts without identifying them as parts of the same universe. There are dozens of naming schema, and no single agreed nomenclature.

But almost all humans will agree on the name of Rho Space. Largely because of its practical value, Rho Space is regarded as something of a known entity, and members of all starfaring races learn about it at a young age. The consensus is unfortunate, because Rho Space doesn't come from any of the logical systems of naming conventions. It wasn't the 17th parallel universe discovered. It was the second or third, but the discoverer selected the name because it was conveniently located before sigma and tau, which were variables in some of his equations. He was an early adopter of the infinite universes theory and felt that they should be named largely at random.

One of the arguments against infinite universes is that, if there really are an infinite number of parallel universes, why have so few been discovered in the thousands of years since the first ones were revealed? One answer to this argument is straightforward: funding for this type of research has dropped off sharply. That's because most of the discovered universes are completely worthless. In most of them, the laws of physics are so radically different that nuclear and chemical reactions don't function at all as they do in our universe. People and machines sent into these universes sometimes drop dead instantly. Other times they burn up. On rare occasions, they turn completely into energy in a massive explosion. Sometimes particles from the other universe leak through and create an even larger explosion. At least three planets have been destroyed in this fashion. Risks like that make investors wary.

And on the other side, the reward could be remarkably small. A few universes are good for setting up "physics pumps," which utilize the differing physical laws to generate energy. But few races utilize this type of power. The leaking disruptions of physical laws are impossible to contain, and they lead to a high risk of catastrophic failure.

But Rho Space is invaluable. It's a tiny, young universe full of diffuse nebulae and no stars. Physics seems to work mostly the same way. At least, ships and people can both enter Rho Space and come out largely unharmed. Most importantly, there seems to be a close correspondence between points in normal space and points in Rho Space. Although the relationship isn't straightforward, the tiny size of the universe means that virtually all points in Rho Space are separated by a much shorter distance than their corresponding points in normal space. When routes are properly calculated, a ship can cross over to Rho Space, cruise at something like a quarter the speed of light for a few hours, then cross back having traversed over 150 lightyears.

Parn could understand all this introductory material reasonably well. However, it didn't help him understand what Ana was doing, or, more importantly, how to help, exhort, or cajole her into doing it faster.

So he decided to visit engineering.

Birque, the engineer, had music piped into the room as he played a game on the terminal. He didn't see Parn when he came in. To get his attention, Parn said, "Engineer, report!"

"What?" Birque startled and jumped. "Oh, Parn, you scared me!" He looked Parn up and down. Then he said, "What're you all dressed up for?"

"I'm the captain, right? Shouldn't I wear the uniform?"

"Well, sure." Birque scratched his head.

"So gimme the report."

"Okay, you got it! Uh . . ." he quickly closed the game and called up the information on the engines. "We're operating at a nominal 30% of capacity, with about 2% of that going to maintaining ship systems and the rest generating thrust. Fuel consumption curves match projections on all the engines . . ." Once he got started, Birque was able to speak extensively and without stopping for hours about the state of the engines. He kept looking for one of the subtle signs captains used to communicate that he should stop, but Parn didn't know how to give those signs, so Birque just kept talking.

Eventually, Parn stopped him with a big wave of his hands. Then he asked Birque to start again at the beginning. This time, Parn stopped him when he first got to something he didn't understand, which was shortly after discussing fuel consumption. Birque did his best to explain, but Parn had a hard time figuring out what he was saying. So Birque recommended a text, and the two of them ate lunch together. Birque explained the text, and, slowly, Parn began to understand. They went back to engineering after lunch and the two of them worked until late.

When Parn returned to his cabin, he found that Ana was asleep with her back to his side of the bed. She had more than two meals' worth of dishes scattered on her desk. Parn got these into the return shaft as quietly as he could manage, and Ana didn't wake up. Then he got his uniform into the return shaft and ordered a clean one for the morning.

When Parn got up, Ana was already awake. She had food and was back at the terminal. Parn realized he was going to have to set an alarm. He cleaned up, put on his new uniform, and headed back down to engineering.

Parn spent three days learning from Birque. At that point, he felt he could understand enough of what Birque was saying about the drives to interpret reports about their function. He hoped that would be enough to make any decisions he needed to make. When they were almost done, Mamillo contacted Parn.

"Saicy's going to be leaving the infirmary today. I think she'd be happy to see you . . . she hasn't had any visitors the last two days."

Parn thought for a moment. "Okay," he said. "Don't release her until I get there." Then he turned back to Birque and they finished the lesson.

Parn took the elevator to the infirmary level. The door opened, and he hesitated before stepping out. Once he started moving, though, he found he moved with purpose. He didn't stop outside the door, but went right in. Saicy was dressed in some of her own clothes—skin-tight, gaudy skirt and a low-cut velvety blouse. Though she had detached them before he arrived, Parn saw the web of muscle conditioners stretched out on the bed below her.

"Parn!" she said. "Don't you cut a fine figure?" She shook her head and smiled appreciatively. "You were the right choice for captain if only for the uniform. The white makes you look so swarthy! Come here!" She gestured.

He walked up beside the bed and she reached out to feel the uniform. She ran her hand along his chest, slipping it under the lapel. Parn cleared his throat and took a half step back. "I'm glad to see you're feeling so much better."

"Oh, I've been better for ages. But that guy," she jerked a thumb at Mamillo, who was diligently working at his desk, apparently oblivious, "is overly cautious. He's already put me off my shooting schedule!"

"Shooting schedule?"

"Sure. You didn't think I was going to be idle this whole trip, did you? No, I've been working hard on production details for our series, and I'd hoped to start shooting yesterday."

Parn looked at her, his eyebrows coming together quizzically.

"You didn't think I was going to wait until I got back to start filming? No, it'd be old news by then. The series has to start now, to strike while the iron is hot, so to speak."

"But how?"

"I've got a studio set up in a room. I have my lines and my action is all blocked out. I just do the scene."

"In a room? By yourself?"

"That's how I shoot half my movies, anyway. You'll see. It'll be great. That is, if that guy ever lets me go."

They both looked at Mamillo. After a pause, he

looked up. "Yeah, fine. Go, as long as he stays with you until you make it to your room."

Saicy looked at Parn.

"Yeah, sure."

"Gimme your arm." She gestured for it as she scooted to the edge of the bed. Her skirt rode up her thighs.

Parn looked away and moved up beside the bed and held out his arm. She slipped her arm in his and used it for support as she slid off the edge of the bed and into her tall shoes. She supported herself briefly as she straightened her skirt with both hands. She grabbed onto Parn just in time to keep herself from falling to the ground.

Parn led her out of the room. She took small steps. He took larger steps—about the smallest he felt comfortable with--but fewer.

By the time they reached her room, her flittery small talk had fallen silent. She was visibly straining, although her makeup concealed any redness in her face and controlled her sweating. She needed all her breath. As the door opened, she puffed, "I think I'm going to postpone shooting today, after all. I don't think I'm up for it."

"Get to it when you can. It can wait. Healing is what matters most now."

"I think you're right," she said, through gritted teeth. "Can you get me to my bed, please?"

The thought of putting Saicy to bed made Parn's blood swell more than the effort of supporting her weight. The two of them headed to the bedroom. At the edge of the bed, Parn turned Saicy around so she was facing him with her back to the bed. He started to lower her down. Midway in the arc, she lost control and sank back on the bed as dead weight. Parn tried to hold her up, but he couldn't. Saicy tried to grab his shoulders to hold herself up, but all she caught was his lapels. He tumbled onto the bed after her. He was barely saved from falling completely onto her by putting his hands out.

Saicy smiled at him. Their faces were too close, and he couldn't see her mouth, but he saw the evidence of it in her eyes. Her perfume climbed into his nostrils. His heart was pounding. "Parn," she said, "you are a fine man."

Parn swallowed. He searched for his voice. Eventually, he found it. "You are a goddess, Saicy. Too sublime for mortal man."

Her smile tilted to one side, narrowing the eye on that side. "It might be nice to be with a mortal man for a change. Not the devils I seem to always end up with." She sighed and her smile faded. "But not today, anyway. I can't even get myself into bed, let alone do anything once I get there."

Parn helped Saicy get her feet into bed. Her legs were silky and smooth, as were her arms, except for where she had been shot. The skin there was rough and flaky, the flesh below pocked by uneven healing. He straightened her a little on the bed, removed her shoes, and put a cover over her. She was asleep before the blanket even fell onto her.

Parn straightened up and looked down at her. Her sensuous curves had been obscured by the blanket. They were now just shapeless lumps. "Just a body," he thought. Then he turned and left.

He went up to the bridge. Urgot quickly shifted the display to be monitoring the thrust. Looking over his shoulder, Parn could understand the data. But he didn't know what Urgot had been doing before. "How are things going?" Parn asked.

He expected something he could easily understand with his new knowledge. But, instead, Urgot grunted. "How's it going? How's it going? Terrible, that's how. Now is the time I'm supposed to be making corrections to put us in the right spot for entering Rho space. But I can't. Because I don't know what the course is supposed to be. I need the course plots, and I need them, now!"

Parn gestured for calm and said, "I'll work with Ana and try to get you the information you need."

Urgot groaned again. He spun around to look directly at Parn. "Frankly," he said, "I don't think she can do it. She's a desk navigator. There's no way she can handle this. I don't know what our other options are, but we don't have much room for error, and it's ticking away every second. If we miss it, we'll have to spin around and take another try, and that could take us several tendays or even several pentads to do. And we'll be at risk again."

Parn sighed and said, shaking his head, "I'll deal with her."

CHAPTER 15

Parn entered the cabin silently. It smelled of stale food, something spicy that he wasn't familiar with. The food itself was sitting in its dish beside the transport bullet. Even from the door, he could see that it was cold, with rivulets of white congealed grease running through the brown viscous sauce. There was a fork in the food, but it didn't look as though more than one bite had been eaten.

Ana groaned. Parn looked at her. Her back was to him, slender shoulders hunched forward, tiny fists raised at the screen. Her thin brown hair was oily and unwashed. Some of it hung down to her neck, but other parts jutted out at strange angles from her head.

Parn looked over her shoulder at the screen. The symbols there were completely alien. He couldn't help her with that. He had to help her with what he could. "Ana," he said.

She spun around and gave a startled yelp. Her surprise quickly turned to anger. "Why are you wearing that?" She thrust her chin at his uniform. "Did you sell the rest of your corer identity to her, too?"

Parn felt the sting. The anger started to well up in him. It was so hot and piercing it would be easy to let himself explode. It would be the easiest thing to do, and something he'd done many times before. He would yell. Break something. Throw something. Threaten her. Maybe even hit her. In this moment, it was tempting to violate even Mamillo's simple advice.

Then he could storm out in his rage. Get drunk or just stay away for a while. He would come back repentant and beg forgiveness for his outburst. Leave the real issue untouched. He'd had a lot of practice with that. What he didn't have a lot of practice with was what he was about to do. "I know you think I sold something that belongs to you or partly belongs to you. And I know that hurt you, even though I don't know how or why. But I'm sorry."

For a moment, her expression started to soften, but then it became hard and angry again. She said something about him being "dumb as lead" and a "stupid mule," but he was too busy seeing to hear most of the words. He was looking at the screen behind her and he was seeing how the anger wasn't coming from her, it was coming from the screen. It was coming through her. And just as it wasn't coming from her, it wasn't directed at him. It was supposed to go through him to hit something else. Maybe the screen again, with its incomprehensible symbols and strange multidimensional shapes.

"I may be stupid dumb, but I know that you can finish this," he pointed at the screen behind her, "and get us to the pepper planet."

Ana scoffed. "That's the dumbest thing you've said since you came in here. You don't even know what that is. And you don't know that I can solve it."

"Yeah, I don't know what it is. But I know we wouldn't be here if it weren't for you." He pointed at the floor, then at her. "You took the initiative to look at the crystal that I never would have had the courage to show you. You had the smarts to figure out what it meant. You had the vision to see that we could put an expedition together, and the knowledge to take us to all those investors. And the stubbornness to not give up, even after all those rejections. And you came up with the plan that took us to Heliopause. And then you made the deal with Saicy." He turned his hands palm up in front of her. "I guess I don't know that you can actually finish this. But based on all that, I can't help but believe that you'll get us there. And I trust you to do it."

"First," Ana said, jabbing her finger angrily at the air, but not pointing directly at Parn, "looking at that crystal wasn't initiative. It was criminal. And anybody in their right mind would've had me locked up at that point. And that would've put an end to our little caper right there. So that's on you."

She turned around more in her chair and gripped the back with both her hands. "And second, if you really trust me to get this done, why are you here?"

Parn came around the bed and sat down on the edge of it. Their faces were so close that he could smell her breath and the unwashed funk coming off her skin. "Because somebody doesn't trust you."

"Who? Urgot? That bastard. That'd be okay, though, cause I don't trust him, either. So that's just fair play." When she saw in his eyes that it wasn't Urgot, she paused. "Oh, don't tell me it's Saicy! That ewe had plenty of time to speak up if she wasn't confident in my ability. You better keep her away from me the rest of this voyage, or, I dunno, I might kill her!"

Parn stopped her rant by putting a hand on one of her flailing arms. The touch jolted him, and though Ana went silent immediately, he was too stunned for a moment to say anything. He felt a smile growing on his face and saw one growing on her face at exactly the same pace.

Ana was laughing when she finally said, "Who?"

"What?" Parn laughed, too.

"Who doesn't trust me?" She pulled her arm away, but the anger was playful now.

"Oh, yeah, sorry." Parn looked down and tried to suppress his smile to get back to the serious mood he was trying to create. "You. You're the one who doesn't trust you."

"What do you mean?"

"Urgot says he needs course corrections from you. I know you've worked them out, but you haven't sent them to him because you don't trust yourself."

A flash of real anger went over her face again. "What are you talking about? Those course corrections are important. And if they're not right, they can put us out of position for when we need to cross over to Rho Space."

"Yeah, I know they're important. And I know what they're for—sorta. But I'm also pretty sure that you've got them done, and they're right. You need to get them to Urgot. He tells me that no course corrections at this point are getting to be as bad as any mistakes you might have made. So get them updated right to this minute and send them to him."

"But—"

"No buts. That's an order."

"Seriously, listen. You don't know what kinds of mistakes I could have made. If I don't get the entry right, we could end up light-years off course with no ability to get back into Rho Space."

"I'm sure you're not light-years off."

She gestured with both hands chopping the air to her right, "But if I err the other way, we could cross back too near the star or a planet. We don't really know what's in that system. I mean, we know there're a couple of gas giants and some rocky planets, but we don't know more than that!"

"So, if you're going to err, err on the outside of the system, but just a little bit. Not so much that we wouldn't be able to get to the system."

"That's a tiny, tiny margin of error."

"Maybe. I dunno about that. But I know you've got it under control. Now send the damn course corrections."

Ana huffed. Then she turned around and worked at the keyboard for a while, sometimes manipulating figures on the screen with a stylus or other devices. Then she paused, sighed, and took two deep breaths. A quick final input and she turned back around. "Okay, that's done."

"Great. Now get cleaned up and we're going to the cafeteria."

"It's the same food they send up here."

"I know, but you need to get out for a little bit. See your shipmates, such as we are."

Birque, Seldon, and Mehany were in the cafeteria. Parn knew that Mamillo rarely left the infirmary, so he wasn't surprised that he wasn't there. Parn also suspected that Urgot was busy trying to translate course corrections into engine burns. He wondered about Saicy, but wasn't worried, yet.

The first burn happened while they were eating. The klaxon sounded for level 1 disruption. Parn explained to Ana that there wasn't much to worry about at that level. They didn't even need to secure their food. The trays were designed to handle it. But when the burn came, it took her by surprise and Parn had to catch her to keep from falling out of the chair—which was secured to the floor.

The burn reminded Mehany about Urgot, and then she started bragging about how she'd beaten him badly in the last few days to close out their table hockey tournament. "He beat me at first because I didn't know him. His reaction time is fast—I have to give him that." She took a big swig of beer, and Parn was reminded how nice it was to be free of the propaganda posters that lined the walls on his corporate voyages. "But he's a coward, and he'd flinch every time I hit the puck real hard. That was enough to let it by."

Parn laughed. He always laughed at Mehany's

stories. But Ana said, "I don't know if that makes him a coward. Just easily startled."

Mehany shrugged. "Maybe. I'm just glad we're not counting on him to be our combat pilot. And I was glad to have him to play. I won a quarter percent of a share off him. That's twice the biggest share I've ever gotten from a corporate voyage."

Seldon said, "That's almost half of what I'm contracted for on this trip. I've never had a share this big." He looked at Parn, "But how much is that really going to mean?"

Mehany turned to Parn, too, "Yeah, do you think this voyage is going to be as lucrative as a corporate one?"

Parn shrugged. He looked in his beer glass, which was unfortunately empty. "Y'know, it always varies, anyway. It depends on if the trees are ripe or not. And how ripe. But if they are ripe, it should be even more profitable. After all, there are fewer of us—and no corporation to take its share. So, if you want, this could be your last coring voyage. You'll probably never have to work again."

"That's what I was hoping for! Maybe I'll get another husband. Or two. I bet I could afford two husbands on that money. Thanks for inviting me."

Mehany raised her glass. Parn raised his, too. Mehany noticed it was empty and recommended a refill.

Parn shook his head. "I have to work." He gestured at his uniform. Then he looked at Ana.

She sighed. "Yeah, I should get back to work, too."

The second burn came while they were in the hallway walking toward the cabin. Again, it wasn't much, but they didn't heed the warning and it was enough to knock Ana sideways into Parn, who caught her. He chuckled, "You'll get better at responding to the burns in time. It just takes practice."

Then they were at the door, and Ana saluted him. "Thanks, Cap'n." She went into the cabin and Parn went up to the bridge.

On the bridge, Parn said to Urgot, "See?"

"Yeah, okay, that's fine for now. But it doesn't mean anything. We won't know if these course corrections are working until it's time to cross over, and then it's too late."

Parn sat down in his chair. "Look, have you ever been on a voyage where the navigator made a bad jump?"

"No . . ."

"Me, neither. Nor has anyone I know."

"That's because people on those trips don't come back."

"Not necessarily. Ana says that a mistake could be just inconvenient."

Urgot rolled his eyes. "Of course she'd say that. Lemme ask you a question. Have you ever been on a voyage with a desk navigator?"

"I dunno. I've never known the navigator on my voyage before."

"Well, I always know the navigator on my voyage. And none of them have been deskers. To hear these guys talk, it's not the same job at all. In theory, a desker could do the same job, given enough time. But you can't just wait around for the time on the ship. You have to have the course ready before it's needed. There's no time to waste."

"I trust her to do her job. Just as I trust you to do yours. Speaking of which: show me how these burns are matching us to the plotted course."

"Not yet."

"Excuse me?" Parn said, his hands going to the arms of his chair.

"No, sorry. What I mean is, there's a burn coming, so let's do it afterward."

"How soon?"

"Very soon."

Sure enough, after a few seconds waiting, the klaxon went off. This burn was very minor. It wasn't necessary to sit for it, Parn thought. As soon as it was finished, he got up and stood at Urgot's shoulder. "Okay, now show me."

Urgot called up the courses. He showed the plotted course and then how the burns were causing them to approach the course. "One more radial burn, then three axials to get us up to speed. Then we wait for the next batch."

"How many course corrections do you normally have on a voyage like this?"

"Normally? Zero. But I don't normally have to dodge an intercepting ship. So . . ." he shrugged.

"Okay, thanks." Parn sat down in the copilot's chair. "Now, show me how you fly this ship."

Urgot seemed to begin a protest, but then he looked into Parn's eyes. He sighed and said, "Fine. Just lemme figure out where to start."

They worked until Urgot was tired and decided to head back to his cabin to rest until the next set of burns. Parn was also feeling exhausted, so he went back to his cabin. Ana was still working. He managed to get her attention, but she said she wanted to keep working. Parn ordered a new uniform for the next day and went to bed.

It went on like this for several days. Parn and Ana made it out to lunch once. The other days, Ana begged work and stayed in, wanting to be undisturbed. A couple of times, Parn tried to coax Ana into taking a break for sex, but she begged work once, and the other time said she was too tired from work. She was working, too—firing off regular course corrections to Urgot—but Parn was also beginning to suspect that maybe some of that anger really had been directed at him.

Parn was also trying to keep up his commitment to learning new things. After a while, Urgot got annoyed at Parn's questions and recommended that he take an automated certification course. If he passed, he would even be certified to take Rafe's place as the backup pilot of record—he'd be able to land the ship—with the computer's help—but he wouldn't be capable of serving as primary pilot. When Parn started the course, Urgot went back to playing a game on the computer. It only took a moment's glance at the screen to confirm that this was what he had been playing several days ago when Parn had first learned about the navigation problem.

But Parn didn't care. The course corrections were being reviewed, adapted, and put into the computer in reasonable time. And, truth be told, he was learning more with the automated course than he'd been able to get under Urgot's disgruntled, irritable tutelage. He was nearing the last lesson of the course when Saicy's series began to arrive.

Parn hadn't seen Saicy much in the days since she got out of the infirmary. When a few days passed, he stopped by her cabin to make sure she was okay. She let him in, wearing a robe with a sparkly dress's skirt trailing underneath. She explained that she was about to shoot a scene and couldn't talk right away. But he could stay to watch, and they could talk afterward. She showed him where to stand, then shrugged the robe off and went into the next room, which had been painted to serve as her digital studio.

If he hadn't guessed from the dress, Parn would immediately have known that she was filming the scene from Heliopause. A robot painted the same color as the room moved around to take the role of other people, and shapes emerged from the floor to mimic stairs, chairs, and a table. Saicy easily put on her vivacious hospitality, playing to the empty room as though it were a crowded bar. She was exactly as he remembered her from that night. The flirty jokes. The big smile that could move from pure enjoyment to conspiratorial faux-scandal with ease. She used her body as she had that night, to tease, reward, or discomfit her patrons in turn. Even though she was acting in a blank room, Parn knew the gestures well enough to know what she was doing just by watching her. And he felt the discomfort of a growing erection.

Despite his discomfort, a quick glance at himself in a mirror positioned at the edge of the studio room showed that the uniform was doing a good job of concealing his response. Good tailoring has its benefits, apparently.

When Saicy finished with her scene, she came out and sat down heavily on the couch in the main room. She let out a deep sigh, then gestured to a chair opposite her. She gave a smile, but it was tired. "Please," she said, simply.

Parn sat down. Although the makeup she wore almost concealed it, Parn could see the exhaustion on her face.

Saicy pulled out a box of assorted parts that Parn soon realized was her assistant. "How can I help you?"

Parn shook his head. "Nothing, really. I just came to make sure you were okay."

Immediately, her face lit up with a smile. Having watched her performance just seconds before, Parn would not swear that it was genuine, but he knew that it felt genuine. He smiled back, full of warmth. "I am, thank you! And so nice of you to come by. I was beginning to fear that you only liked me in the role of damsel in distress. Or that you were coming here to talk about that annoying pay dispute between your corer friend and the pilot." She she turned her attention partly to the assistant.

"Huh? What dispute?" Parn leaned forward.

Saicy gestured dismissively with the soldering iron. "Your friend is trying to get me to alter the original terms of the contract to reflect their little bet. I told them I can't do that. If they want to get that payment arrangement changed, they have to sign a contract between them. Unfortunately, since they didn't sign the contract before starting the games, there's no binding way to force the pilot to give over the money. I think he's going to renege, personally."

Parn signed. "That wouldn't surprise me. But how is your show going so far? Watching you perform was fun—you were amazing!"

"Thank you," Saicy said. Her smile faded slightly. "It's going fine. It's hard to keep up the level of energy in two g's that I had in one and change. Add my injury to that, and it's pretty exhausting. But the interest levels should be about peaking at the time we release the first episode, so I think it's going to be great. I've also got a lot of requests for commercials—really profitable in the long run, but right now it seems like just another task." Suddenly she looked up, her smile growing very large again. She pointed the iron at Parn and jabbed it at the sky for emphasis. "Hey, I've got an idea. Do you think you could persuade Ana to shoot a commercial for the mecha company? It would make them happy and it would free up some time in my shooting schedule."

"I can try." Parn rubbed his chin. "But I don't think she'd want to."

"Too bad," Saicy shrugged, then turned her attention back to working on her assistant.

The conversation was largely over at that point, but Parn managed to continue with some pleasantries until he could politely excuse himself.

Parn didn't know what to expect from the series, and when it came out, it turned out that it was much better than Parn had feared—and much worse.

When he saw the series, he marveled at how well it was put together. He would never have imagined that Saicy was millions of miles away from her costars. On the other hand, the series itself was a million miles away from where he was. For as much as watching Saicy act had felt exactly as it had the night he was at Heliopause, the series was nothing like his life had been.

Ana's character was not named after her. She was named Biere. Completely reimagined. She was a dumpy, shrewish woman who never believed in Parn's "dream." The first few minutes of the first episode showed that she had been stringing him along while his money lasted, getting him to spend the last of it to take her out to the fancy club, where she had supposedly arranged a meeting with a high-profile investor who was interested. But there was no meeting, and after Parn revealed he was practically broke, she dumped him. Parn used the last of his money to buy a drink, and as he was nursing it, Saicy came up. She recognized him right away as someone who was different from the other men in the place, and she became interested. The two stayed in the bar until after everyone left, at which point, Parn broke down and told her about the pepper planet.

She decided to invest, and they assembled the crew more or less as it had happened. But then it turned out that Biere had illegally (and, Parn knew, impossibly) made a copy of the navigation crystal, and was working with a version of Astreyan named Gurtok. They had a mixed-species crew of scoundrels that they were going to use to board Saicy's ship (an elegant space yacht) and kill her, Parn, and their all-human crew. The entire plot worked predictably toward a climactic spaceship battle intercut with hand-to-hand combat in the yacht. Parn ended up taking Ana's epic turn in the mecha, saving Saicy not from a combat robot, but from a towering, lascivious Gurtok.

But the worst part about it was the heavy-handed romantic tension that was set up between Parn and Saicy. The two were obviously into each other, but they couldn't ever get together—something always came up. It was predictable and tiresome, but also embarrassing. It became a joke around the ship. Mehany thought she was just being funny when she teased him, but it made Parn feel terrible. Birque also didn't realize what he was doing when he mocked Parn.

Ana, on the other hand, supposedly didn't have time for anything but work, except that she somehow managed to fit episodes in. Parn could tell because of how she acted after each episode released. After a while, Parn gave in and stopped trying to talk to her. Instead, he went to the bridge to work on his courses some more. He knew that Urgot was silently mocking him, but at least it was silent.

When the season finale came, all that romantic tension had release. Parn and Saicy made passionate love. Parn watched red-faced, as his replacement character pawed Saciy onscreen. The worst part was that it featured his actual words to Saicy about her being a goddess and her reply about devils. It sounded so ridiculously overwrought that it made him blush even worse. Plus, the line kept getting thrown back at him all day.

Ana was livid, but there was no time to discuss the mess Parn had created by selling his story. They were reaching the crossover point, and it was time to find out whether Parn or Urgot was right about her ability as a navigator.

CHAPTER 16

Like most corers, Parn liked to pass the time in Rho Space safely sedated. For although Rho Space was safe to pass through, it wasn't pleasant. You could feel the irregular space passing through your body. All the distances between the various parts of your body were being compressed, expanded, and otherwise distorted by the voyage. Over the timespan of hours, the effects weren't permanent for a living being. Your body would usually put itself back together. But if you took too many trips too quickly, you would suffer. In rare cases, less flexible tissues like teeth and bones cracked.

Ships always experienced a certain amount of "jump fatigue" with each trip. Any ship spending more than an hour in Rho Space had to undergo a complete inspection during its next visit to port.

And most ships had a hard upper limit of Rho Space hours on the order of a few hundred. Their current ship had spent about eighty hours in Rho Space against its rated maximum of 250. After that, it was believed that every component in the ship would be so warped that it was safer and more cost-efficient to scrap the ship and replace it. Corporations didn't like to push that limit, though, as the odds of a spontaneous ship failure increased dramatically as you approached three-quarters of the rated maximum. So they sold these "Rho-rated" ships to wildcatters.

Purchasing a Rho-rated ships had been one of Parn's original plans for his expedition. He didn't like the risk, but thought he'd have to endure it. They were available for a tiny fraction of the cost of a new ship. Saicy had the money to buy a ship that had spent a lot fewer hours in Rho Space and so was safer.

As captain, Parn couldn't be sedated through Rho Space. Now, as he felt the tensions of Rho Space contorting his tissues, Parn was glad to be in a ship he felt was probably safe against these distortions. He clenched his teeth and fists against the pain but pushing against himself created a strange resonance that he hated. He wanted to scream, but he was terrified what that would sound like. The hours stretched on, and Parn thought for a long time that it just wasn't going to end. And then it did.

Coming, out, Parn groaned and trembled. His muscles felt like he'd been boxing fifteen rounds without a break: burning with lactic acid and aching with bruises. But the pain didn't stop there: it went deep into his bones. He wondered how people didn't get cancer from Rho Space. Then he realized that they probably did. They said if you didn't do it too often, you were safe, but that's the sort of convenient lie that would become institutionalized.

Parn wanted to crawl off and go to bed. But he had a few things to do first. "System check?"

Urgot replied, "Just completed. Some minor system failures, but in every case, the backups kicked in just fine. Repairbots dispatched. Looks like a couple backup systems burned out, too, but the primaries are still running. Adding those to repair queues."

"Okay, check our position."

"Gravity field is right. Radiation indicates that

we're exactly at the heliopause. And sighting stars confirm that we're around the star we wanted."

"Great." Parn tried to swallow, but his mouth was dry. He tried moving his tongue around to stir up some saliva, but that just hurt, and he was still parched. "Is there a planet in the pepper zone?"

"We're still waiting on gravimetrics. The computer's isolated two gas giants. One rocky planet outside the pepper zone . . . And one inside the pepper zone!" Urgot's excited gesture got cut off midway by a wince.

Parn settled for a sigh, but even that hurt. Smiling hurt, too, but he couldn't help himself. "Okay. Thanks, Urgot. Mark a course, but put it on delay. Give yourself enough time to get to bed before deceleration starts." Parn knew that gravity would increase his pain a hundredfold. He unfastened himself and drifted to the ladder. He thought that using the ladder would be less painful than fighting the elevator's acceleration and deceleration.

When Parn entered the cabin, he was surprised when Ana turned to look at him. He had expected her to be asleep still. But looking at her bloodshot, sunken eyes, he wouldn't have been surprised if the sedative hadn't worked at all. "Are we there?"

"Yes. Your course was perfect. And there's a possible pepper planet!"

Ana went from almost comatose to squealing projectile in nothing flat. Parn put up his hands to block her, but when she hit him, his entire body exploded in pain. As she pushed off the bathroom doorframe to send them spinning through the air, Parn wanted to cry. He just managed a whimper.

"Oh, I'm sorry," Ana said, and it was clear that her own pain had caught up to her. "Yeah, ouch. And I heard that it's worse if you're awake. Is it worse?"

Parn gave a slight nod. "Much worse."

"Sorry."

"It's okay. Let's get to bed. We're going to be decelerating soon, and I want to be in bed for that."

Ana came up against the bulkhead first, so she pushed them toward the bed about as gently as she could, then settled him onto the bed. She tucked them both in, her arm across his chest and her eyes looking into his.

Parn said, "Y'know, when the engines kick in, your arm is gonna weigh a ton and it's gonna hurt like hell."

"Oh, sorry." She said, and moved her arm off

him. She was laying at his side, their arms parallel and touching.

"Let's have enough space so that we don't touch even when the gravity flattens us out."

She moved over slightly. "Like that?"

"Yeah. Also, I want to be sedated." He put a dose into his drug port. His pain immediately began to diffuse, and his mind started to unfocus. "I may be asleep, and we may not even be touching, but I want you to know the three things I'm feeling right now."

"Tell me."

"One: pride. I knew you could do it, and you showed everyone you could. You are amazing."

Ana smiled. "What's two?"

"Smugness. I knew you could do it when no one else did. Not even you. I am amazing."

She made a fake pout and then smiled at him again. "Okay . . . do I even want to know three?"

"Love. I love you so much, and I can't imagine anything changing that." Ana smiled even more broadly. She reached out two fingers and touched his hand. He didn't feel any pain. Just a slight pressure and warmth. Then she withdrew them. As he drifted away, Parn wasn't sure how much of the joy he felt was love and how much was drugs. He wasn't sure it mattered, so he called it all love. It was all love, and the pain was gone.

CHAPTER 17

Urgot plotted them a generous course to the potential pepper world. Generous in that it allowed them to decelerate more slowly. Although Parn slept for the first fifteen hours or so of deceleration, he appreciated it when he woke up. One and a half gees were definitely gentler on his sore muscles and bones. And it made making love to Ana considerably easier.

While Parn appreciated the lower deceleration, he didn't like the extra time required to make orbit. After the first few days, Parn was unhappy with the thought of waiting sixty days to make orbit and see if the planet actually had pepper trees on it.

And it wasn't just Parn. Everyone was impatient with having to wait so long to reach the planet. Saicy was particularly troublesome. She was cut off from her media, so she had to do something. She flirted with Birque and Urgot, giving them each her favor in turns, then setting them jealously against one another.

To stop it, Parn set Saicy to work as an apprentice to Mehany, learning how to prep the spiderbots for harvesting. Parn wasn't sure this was a good strategy. Although Mehany was generally a good worker, she also had a mischievous streak, and Parn worried that Saicy would tap into that. So he decided to check in on them after a few days without hearing what was happening.

He was surprised when he was met at the door by a spiderbot. It barred his way with its massive rounded body and four strong arms, then said. "Please wait here while I announce you."

The voice struck Parn as familiar, but he couldn't link it to any of the spiderbots he had worked with. Each bot was different, and you worked with them for such an intense period, you came to know them as well as any of your fellow corers, except for the fact that you never saw them between voyages.

The spiderbot turned its knob-like head,

bristling with sensors, and called out, "Parn is here to see you, ma'am."

Saicy called out, "Be a dear and let him in, please, Cap."

The voice was Saicy's assistant's. He watched the spiderbot with wonder as it gestured for him to enter, then dropped to all ten legs to escort him to where Saicy and Mehany were deep in the guts of a spiderbot.

Parn jerked his thumb at the spiderbot. "How . . . and why did you rebuild the bot into your assistant?"

Saicy sighed. "Those men wouldn't leave us alone. I swear, if Birque or Urgot burst in here one more time, I was gonna shit a quasar. So I needed some way to keep them out."

Mehany chuckled, "And she was afraid I was going to hurt them."

Saicy laughed. "Oh, yes, I saw it in her eyes. She might've killed one! And then where would we be? The fines for returning without a legal complement are astronomical unless you can prove exigent circumstances—and I don't think overexuberant protectress counts."

Parn laughed, too. He looked into the women's

twinkling eyes. They had been sharing secrets as they worked, and now they were sharing private jokes back and forth. Parn couldn't think what they might be, so he kept to the main conversation. "That was smart. I have seen her put some serious hurt on people. But how did you modify the spiderbot?"

"Oh, it was easy! You know I'd been trying to repair my assistant ever since the unfortunate incident with the protection robots. But the hardware was too damaged, and we didn't have all the spare parts. I'd been improvising, but it was slow going, and the results were fragile and unreliable at best. But when I started working on the spiderbot, I realized how simple it was to isolate the proper part of the code related to the robot's personality and function, then replace it with my assistant's code, and, boom, a functioning assistant who is also strong enough to hold the men at the door."

"I'd'a thought you might be done with bodyguard robots after what happened with the last ones." Parn sat down on a stool across the table from the women. He'd never rated training in this part of the job, so he didn't understand any of what he was looking at.

Saicy waved her hand dismissively, "I tell you what: I'm done with off-the-shelf security protocols. I programmed my assistant myself, so I know she's safe. Those others? They assured me they were safe, but I should've known better. Not interfering with the hardware or software of the robots was part of the promotional deal. I should've walked away, but the money was too good."

"And in the end, the money turned out to be real good, didn't it?" Mehany laughed.

"Yeah," Saicy smiled, "It did."

"All's well that ends well . . ." Mehany said.

"Except for Rafe," Parn said.

Saicy frowned deeply. "I'm sorry about your friend."

Now Mehany waved dismissively. "Don't be too sorry. Rafe was kind of an asshole and kind of a scum, too." She gestured at Parn with her wrench. "Plus he was never smart enough to know what to do in a crisis. If he'd just looked to you when things started to go wrong, he'd've made it out like the rest of us."

Parn was quiet. He didn't know what to say about that. Mehany looked at him confidently. He couldn't help glancing at Saicy, who he was sure would look through him as the fraud he was. But she looked at him with the same confidence as she absently rubbed her arm where she had been shot. He couldn't understand her look—mostly what he remembered from when the robots went crazy was panicking and following her direction into the escape tunnel. And he remembered Rafe's death as coming during that time of panic and confusion, possibly because of his panic and confusion. The rest of it was a blur to him. There was nothing in his memory to justify any statements of confidence.

The silence lingered, and he realized they expected him to say something. He hit his leg with his fist. "Let's just hope the rest of us make it home safely."

"With lots of pepper!" Mehany said, hitting his shoulder and smiling without a hint of melancholy.

"Yeah," Parn said, scratching his ear. "That reminds me why I came down here, after all. The robots will be ready in time for landing?"

"You bet." Mehany gestured at the bay of spiderbots. "We've just got a couple more to get ready. And here's the really good news: it was only corporate policy that required a bot and a person to harvest together. These robots are fully capable of harvesting on their own. So we could double our operation, or just have the bots harvest instead of us!"

Parn rebelled at the thought. The robot could probably harvest faster than he could and more accurately, but he knew he would do it better. "We'll talk about that. There was probably a good reason why the companies paired humans and robots together in harvesting." He sighed. "Besides, we're still not even sure there'll be pepper to harvest."

Saicy smiled. She patted Parn's cheek. "Don't be so pessimistic! Ana said the odds were good. I'm confident that there'll be pepper."

"Yeah, you're probably right. And we'll be ready to harvest it."

Parn took his leave and headed up to the infirmary. Having completed his certification as a secondary pilot, he was working with Mamillo to learn some basic medical techniques. The certification process for a secondary medical officer was much more extensive than for a pilot, so he didn't think he'd be able to complete it, but he wanted to try.

As he was leaving the infirmary, Urgot stopped him in the hall. "Hey," the pilot said, his voice as abrupt as his arm on Parn's shoulder, "you need to do something about her."

"Who?"

"Saicy. That ewe has her robot stopping me from seeing her."

"That's her business, not mine. But I'll give you a word of advice. If she doesn't want to see you, you should know well enough to leave her alone. She shouldn't need the robot to keep you out."

"No, man, you don't understand. She made me promises. And I did stuff for her, and now she's cut me off cold. That's not right."

"Promises, like a contract? As captain, I can mediate a contract dispute."

"No, man, you know chicks like that. They always making promises." Urgot made a gesture with his hands as if he were grabbing two globes.

"Oh. That. I can't help you with that. But I advise you again to just let it go."

Parn started to move past, but Urgot stopped him again. "I seen the way you look at her. You feel like I do. She's made promises, and we can make her pay. You, me, and Birque. She shouldn't be allowed to play us like chumps."

Parn looked hard at Urgot. "I must be misunderstanding you, because surely you're not suggesting what it sounds like you're suggesting." He tried to stand as tall and as straight as he could manage, trying to be every inch the captain he was supposed to be.

Urgot scoffed. "Yeah, maybe you are a chump. But debts always come due."

"Please, focus on the planet. We'll soon be in range to sight for pepper trees, right?"

"Yeah, yeah, yeah. Soon." Urgot waved dismissively and headed toward the elevator.

Parn didn't want to spend any more time with Urgot, so he went to the ladder, even though climbing it in this gravity was painful. And when he got to the ladder, he decided he wanted to check in on Birque.

When he asked him about Saicy, Birque flushed and lowered his head shamefully. "I know, I know. I shoulda stopped when she said to leave her alone. But it was so nice when we were hanging out, I thought maybe if I could just say things the right way, it would persuade her to spend more time with me. But I got the idea now. That robot was the hint I needed. I'm gonna leave her alone."

"You'd better," Parn commanded. "And while you're at it, stay away from Urgot."

Birque looked up at the name. "Now that guy." He grunted and made a fist. "I don't even know what to say about him."

"You don't have to say anything. Just stay away from him. Obviously a touchy situation, and we're so close that I don't want anything to mess up the expedition. Right?"

Birque nodded.

"And if he comes to you, you tell him that I said you're supposed to stay apart. If he has anything to say, he can say it to me."

Birque rubbed his chin. "Okay."

Parn felt he had stamped out a potential fire there, but he was very happy when they were approaching critical distance to scout the planet for pepper trees. That would refocus everyone on the central point of the mission.

Everyone gathered in the rec room, the only room where they could all watch the external feed together. Ana stood next to Parn, and as the first images came in, she slipped her hand into his.

Knowing that people would expect him to say something, Parn had practiced what to say as the images came in. He gestured with his free hand and spoke. "First images look good. Temperate, terrestrial world, ideal for pepper seeds to take root. Just like Ana predicted."

She gave his hand a squeeze.

"Haze of an atmosphere. Light blue indicating oxygen, so that's a good sign. The probe is sweeping around the planet to make a survey. Looks like in the night side there's an equatorial land mass—perfect."

Ana bounced a little. There were excited murmurs all around.

"This is laser imagery: it's all false color, indicating the height of vegetation. At that height, those could be stage one trees, but maybe not—there are plenty of indigenous trees that height. But, wait, those scattered high ones, those have to be stage two trees."

Ana started to jump, and Parn was barely quick enough to stifle the excited reaction.

"Scattered like that is not a good sign. It means the grove is too young." A collective sigh and some nervous shuffling. Then Parn gasped as the entire screen changed color. He pointed emphatically, "But that's got to be a mature grove! Too dense to be anything but. We've got pepper!"

The entire room erupted. Ana was the first to hug and kiss him, but she was by no means the last. Parn barely took notice. He was just relieved.

CHAPTER 18

As the equatorial continent moved into daylight, the probe reconfigured and dove into the atmosphere to get a treetop perspective. It sent back images of hard, sleek seed pods atop the towering stage two trees. They had attained the shiny, resinous black luster of ripeness. The sepals had even started curling back, revealing the rocket-like shape of the pods. Parn knew the similarity to primitive rockets continued deeper into the plants where the seed pods had stabilizing fins.

When the pepper exploded, the bark would channel the force upward. The sepals would fall away, and the seed pod would rise. Pods at this stage of development were the final proof that there was pepper, and lots of it. Thousands of stage two trees spread across the continent, surrounded by an even larger grove of stage one trees.

The next challenge was landing. It was vital to glide down to the landing site without using thrust, because that could ignite the trees. And once the trees had started to burn, it was only a matter of time before they detonated, consuming the pepper and sending the seeds into space.

This is where Urgot proved his worth. After the probe had identified a potential site near the stage one trees, Urgot worked with the computer to plot a gliding course that would plant them gently at the site. Then he worked with the computer to execute the course against the unpredictable winds. Parn assisted, but he was able to offer only minimal help. In the end, a small burn was necessary just at the last to keep the landing gear within safety tolerances.

Then Parn, Mehany, and Saicy emerged quickly to put out the small fires that had begun. Saicy's mecha was adapted with firefighting gear and moved quickly to quell the largest blazes. Parn and Mehany moved slower to perform a more detailed sweep and address the smoldering hotspots, working around the large, flat toes of the ship's landing gear.

After the first flurry of activity, Parn and Mehany took off their gas masks. The atmosphere was mostly safe. Just trace outgassing from the stage two trees and some smelly but mostly harmless thiols. When Ana came out to bring them lunch, she marveled both at the height of the stage one trees and at the smell of the air, which drove her back inside shortly. The corers stayed outside until all traces of fire were gone, and the ship's hull had cooled to a safe temperature. Meanwhile, Saicy scouted the area around the stage one grove. The grove itself was too dense for her mecha to easily penetrate, but the scrub savanna around it was easy to traverse. The lush green grass was so tall that the driver compartment was just barely visible over the seedheads.

Parn looked at the stage one trees and noted how clearly alien they were from the native grass. The trees had distinctly red-brown leaves whose photosynthetic structures were completely different from the grasses that gave them a wide berth. The trees had a superficial resemblance to conifers, but instead of needles, they had long flat hexagonal leaves that hooked together in bright light to form solid plates. The roots looked alien, too. Instead of just coiling over and under one another, they linked together, creating a network that made it easier to collect nutrients and food, then send these to the stage two trees.

By the time Saicy returned, the sun was low in the sky and everyone went inside to plan the next day's activities. Parn consented to let their extra spiderbots go harvesting on their own, but he insisted that he be there when they started to test the pepper so he could make sure the robots were "doing it right."

So the next morning, Parn, Mehany, and Seldon set out with six spiderbots. Mehany and her bot went off to a nearby tree. Parn tested the quality of pepper on a couple of trees and set the independent spiderbots on them, planning to come back in a few hours. Then he took his bot off to a likely tree. As he headed off, he thought he saw a number of stone shelves like the tops of buildings. They looked too square and too level to be natural formations. But if they were buildings of some sort, the civilization that made them must be long gone. They were surrounded by stage one pepper trees, which meant that the soil was too toxic for any crops that would be edible for anything that could breathe this atmosphere. The old stories replayed in his mind. Pepper gods. Space mermaids. Grand old civilizations noble but dying or at least doomed to execution by the presence of star pepper. He sighed and put it out of mind, focusing on selecting a likely pepper tree.

When he tested the pepper of his chosen tree, he smiled. It had a delicate, rose-like scent underneath the layers of organic solvents. And it was really ripe. All this grove needed was some tiny event to set it off. And then the entire grove would detonate in a consuming fiery apocalypse from which only the pepper pods would emerge. All the more reason to harvest them as soon as possible.

It was time to get to work. Parn was shocked at how easily he fell back into the old rhythm. Cutting bricks, bagging them, handing them over to the spiderbot was all as natural as breathing. He lost track of time and was only brought back into awareness of it when his timer signaled a mandatory break at six hours. He stepped outside and ate a tasteless protein bar sitting on the spiderbot's rounded body, held safely in by several of the arms, which formed a cage around him. He was near enough to the edge of the stage two tree grove that he could see through them to the lower stage one trees, and even past them to the waving grass and the choppy sea. The sun was high in the sky. The air was hot and humid. It was a beautiful world, and Parn thought briefly how sad it was that it would be destroyed when the pepper plants exploded. When his break ended, he went back to work, but the thought troubled him.

At his next break, it was dark outside, but only recently dark. He could see a line of light on the western horizon. The rest of the land and sea were dark, except for the area where the ship's lights were visible even though the ship itself was hidden behind the trees. And then another cluster far off to the south. His heart sank. It looked like it might be a fire.

Even a small grass fire might be enough to set off the outgassing from the trees if it got close enough. But a grass fire didn't make sense. He remembered the lush greenness of the grass he had seen. It shouldn't be susceptible to a self-sustaining fire. And the fire didn't look like it was spreading. Using the range-finding equipment in his helmet, he determined it was far enough from the forest that it wouldn't be a danger. Still, it was a mystery and deserved to be investigated. But he wasn't equipped to do that, so he made a note in his computer and put it out of his mind when his break ended.

At the time of his next break, it was full dark. He looked up at the alien sky and tried to remember how many times he'd harvested pepper for the corporations. All those alien worlds for someone else's profit. Now he was earning his own profit. That was nice, but what he was really enjoying was just being able to do the harvesting again. And living up to his commitment to Vigar. Looking up at the stars, he wondered if people had immortal souls as some believed. Would the soul get peace or satisfaction from Parn's accomplishment or was the reward for him alone?

He wondered what kind of reward might make Vigar satisfied. Was it just the money? Vigar had never really valued money too highly. He had valued the corer's craft, and Parn tried to honor that commitment. Parn felt irritation again at letting the spiderbots harvest on their own. But the compromise seemed in keeping with some of Vigar's other values. He had the kindness to take the inexperienced corer Parn under his wing. And the generosity to share with Parn and others when they needed it. He was also generous with his acquired wisdom, teaching Parn what he needed to survive as a corer. Parn resolved to make sure this expedition honored those values of Vigar's.

Then he remembered about the fire. He scanned all around but didn't see it. Must've gone out on its own. So he put it out of mind and went back to work.

On his next break, he got a communication from Mehany. "Hello?" he said.

"Oh, good, you're alive. We were starting to get worried."

"Really? Why?"

"You've been gone a long time. Remember, you're not working for the corporation now. You don't have to put in these long hours."

"I know. But this is just my rhythm. It seems wrong to come back early. Besides, the pepper will dry out if I leave."

Mehany scoffed. "Let it. We have so few corers on this trip, there's no risk that we'll run out of easily accessible pepper even if we only harvest half a chamber."

Parn was annoyed again. That was not how things were done: when you opened a chamber, you harvested all the pepper. Parn knew if he started talking to Mehany about doing things "the right way," she would just get annoyed and defensive, so he said, "I like to work this way."

"Okay, but if you do start to get really tired, remember that you can stop at any time. It's your choice."

"I will, thanks."

And then Parn climbed back into the tree. For the first time it occurred to him that other people might not love working to complete exhaustion the way he did. Their loss.

It was not quite full dark when Parn reached the end of his shift. His muscles were sore, his vision blurred, and he felt a little like he was floating. But he still noticed the fire again in roughly the same place as before. He made a note of it, then ordered the spiderbot to take him home.

The spiderbot didn't drop Parn at the entrance ramp. Instead, it climbed to the upper cargo hold, the first they were loading with pepper. After logging his harvest, Parn extended a ladder to the crew ramp, since that's where the locker room was. He washed up and headed up to his cabin, too tired to mention the fires he had sighted. Ana was already asleep when he entered. He climbed into bed beside her, happy that she had warmed the bed for him. It was almost exactly like falling into a bunk that had been vacated by another corer just moments before. But it smelled nicer.

When he woke, Parn found he'd slept late. By the time he was dressed and having breakfast, everyone else had already eaten and was well into their routines for the day. After eating alone for a while, he picked up his tray and went in search of someone to talk to.

He found Ana and Saicy outside practicing with the mecha in the long afternoon shadows of the stage one trees. Saicy was teaching Ana how to operate it in uneven terrain and how to take advantage of some of its more advanced features. Parn was surprised at first to see a spiderbot hanging out behind Saicy. Then he realized it had the same deferential puppy attitude as her assistant, and he remembered she had reprogrammed it. For her part, Ana was consenting to some promotional images that could be used in a future advertising campaign for the mecha. She had the canopy open for one of these shots when she noticed Parn. She called to him and waved, then frantically began working at the safety straps. After a couple of seconds without progress, she made a frustrated grunt.

Saicy looked over her shoulder at Parn and gave him a smile. Then she turned back to Ana and said, "Here, let me." She got up on a step on the mecha's leg, her tight skirt stretching over the active muscles in her buttocks and legs. She had Ana free in a second.

Ana bounded down the mecha and barely touched the ground between it and Parn. She threw herself on him, and his breakfast tray almost went tumbling. Between kisses, she said, "I was so worried! I had no idea you'd be gone so long, and then when Mehany and Seldon came back, but you didn't for hours and hours, oh, I didn't know what to do."

"Ha-ha. I'm sorry. I didn't mean to worry you. It just never occurred to me that you might not know what to expect." He gestured with his fork toward the mecha, "Still, it seems like you found something to do."

"Oh, yeah," Ana said, scratching her head. "I finished our Rho Space plot back to Xythas, so I don't have a lot of work to do on the ship right now. So Saicy offered to teach me this."

"I'm glad to see the two of you are friends."

Ana waved dismissively. "We aren't friends. But I can work with her now. That was mostly just me being nervous. I never thought I'd have to recalculate a course on the fly like that. I wasn't prepared."

"Hm, yeah. Hey, you wanna do something real with the mecha? Investigate this fire I saw from my tree." He sent them the pictures of the fire from his perch. His computer had already extrapolated the location of the fires—it was the same—so it would be easy to check out with a ground-eating mecha.

"I don't know . . ." Ana said. "That sounds like it could be dangerous."

"It won't be dangerous in the mecha," Saicy said. Her interruption startled both Parn and Ana. She smiled sheepishly and came forward, stepping gingerly over the root-hummocked ground. Her breasts bounced in her half-open blouse. "The mecha can handle anything you're going to run into on this planet. Most animals won't be able to harm you, and you can outpace anything big enough to be a threat. The drones will warn you about anything you need to watch out for. And if you get into trouble, you'll be able to shoot your way out."

Ana shrugged and said, "I dunno. Maybe. I'd have to get more confident in it." Then she gestured at Saicy. "Why don't you do it? You're obviously the expert in the mecha."

Saicy twisted her shoulders, slanted her mouth, and made a dismissive wave of her hand. "I suppose. It does all the work. You don't have to be an expert, really. But I don't want to go gallivanting all over the countryside. I've got some projects here that I want to work on."

"Oh?" asked Parn. "And what would those be?"

Saicy smiled and shrugged in a gesture of innocence. "Look who's so curious all of a sudden. It's nothing too big. I'm just into it right now. Besides, don't you have some star pepper to harvest?"

"No," Ana said, grabbing Parn by the lapels of his half-open jacket. "Not now. Now I've got a project I want him to work on."

Letting himself be pulled around, Parn said, "Oh? And what would that be?"

Ana did a little imitation of Saicy's gesture.

"Look who's so curious all of a sudden." Then she became herself and gave Parn a come hither gesture. "Come inside and find out."

After sex, Ana pressed her sweaty body against Parn's. He was grinning stupidly, but her expression was serious. "You could have sex with Saicy," she said. "It's come up that she'd be willing, and, I-I'd be okay with that."

"Naw," said Parn. "I don't think I'd want that."

Ana pushed herself away from Parn. Her voice rose. "You don't have to lie to me. I've seen how you look at her. It's obvious you want her."

"Yeah, well, obviously, I want to look. Who wouldn't? She's got the most beautiful body. And, I mean, maybe if it were just us on a voyage like this, we could definitely have something like Mehany and I had—"

Now Ana sat bolt upright. "Wait, you had sex with Mehany? Mehany? And you expect me to believe you don't want to have sex with Saicy?"

Parn sat up, too, and raised his hands defensively. "Woah. Be calm. Yeah, Mehany and I had sex. Quite a few times when we were on harvesting trips together. But it wasn't anything. Just passing time, something friends do between card games.

And, yeah, I could definitely do that with Saicy, if she'd really be up for it and you weren't here. But why would I have sex with her when I can have sex with you?"

Ana looked at him, slant-eyed and suspicious. "Because she's beautiful."

"Yeah, but you're beautiful, too. And I love you." Now he moved closer, enfolding her in his arms. "So excuse me if I like to look at Saicy, because it's you I really want to touch." He kissed her.

She kissed back, pushing him down onto the bed with the force of her lips. "Prove it."

Parn slept well that night, and when he woke up in the morning, he was deeply refreshed. Ana wasn't in the room. Parn got up and went to his wardrobe. He was tempted to put on the captain's uniform and wander around the ship for the day. But he also felt a driving compulsion when he looked at his coring clothes. So he put them on. He would head out for another long harvesting session.

First, he inspected the lots harvested by the lone spiderbots. He found them technically flawless, but also felt that they were somehow soulless.

He was surprised to find Saicy in the hold, sipping coffee and staring at the stacked and bound bundles of star pepper. She seemed hypnotized, but when he stepped between her and the stacks, it broke her concentration.

"Parn," she said, her voice less assured than usual, "is that all . . . star pepper?"

Parn nodded.

She whistled. "Wow . . . and you can fill this whole room with it?"

Parn nodded again, saying, "If we have enough time. Sometimes we have to cut operations short, but usually we leave with all the holds full."

Her smile grew bigger. "I'm going to make a fortune." Then she turned to Parn. "Ana and I were going to have breakfast, then she wanted to learn more about the mecha. Last time she was concerned you weren't getting enough to eat on your shift. You should eat with us."

Parn agreed.

Ana met them at the cafeteria. She had barely a second glance for Saicy, and didn't ask what the two of them were doing together.

As they were getting ready to leave, Urgot entered the cafeteria. He gave Saicy a dark glare, but she was unfazed. Outside, Parn activated his spiderbot and headed out to the tree he had been working on last time.

Parn found working on the tree as enjoyable as before. He started out thinking about Ana and all the pleasures she gave him, but soon he stopped thinking about anything but the simple act of carving and packing the pepper. The hours passed blissfully.

But at his first break, Mehany contacted him. "I think you need to come back. Don't do such a long shift—we need you here."

"Why?"

"I'm not sure what's going on, but it feels like something's changed. Saicy's acting different, and Urgot, he's being more of an asshole than usual. He's acting more like he's in charge. I think we need you here to help rein him in."

Parn said, "I don't know what I could do that you can't."

"You're the captain."

"Yeah, I guess." Parn looked away from the setting sun and saw a bright green star. As he focused on it, he realized that it wasn't a star. It might be a planet. And then he remembered that Ana had said there were possibly two pepper planets in this system. That could be the other one.

"Parn!"

"What? Oh, I don't know what to do. Lemme just finish this shift. I'll think about the problem and come back with a solution."

Mehany sighed. "You'd better."

"Trust me, I will." He said, then disconnected. But he didn't think of anything. He lost himself in the harvest again.

CHAPTER 19

When Parn got back after his long shift, he could feel something was wrong, but he was too tired to do anything about it. He was accosted first by Birque, then by Mehany. Birque he was able to send off with a wave and a stern glance, but Mehany wouldn't go so easily.

She could clearly see that he wasn't in a state to do anything right now, but she put her hand on his arm. "Tomorrow, put on your captain's uniform and do something."

"Yeah, yeah," Parn said.

In his cabin, Ana was waiting for him. Parn tried to stop her with his gaze, but she wouldn't be swayed. "Parn, Parn, it's so amazing!"

"Huh?"

"I took the mecha out just like you said. And

that fire you saw, it's people! I mean, aliens, but they're intelligent. And that's their village. They were bewildered when I showed up, but they seem like they'd be friendly. You have to come see them!"

Parn admitted that it was exciting, but he was too tired to talk about it. "I'll go see them tomorrow."

But in the morning, Parn first put on his captain's uniform and walked the ship. He visited Birque, who complained that Urgot had come in and demanded that the engines be put into the liftoff configuration.

"Is there a problem with that?"

"What? No. I mean, they're designed to be ready in that position, but I hadn't gotten around to it. I was gonna, but then he came in and told me I had to."

"And did you do it?"

"Yeah, I mean, it's a good idea. In case we have to liftoff fast. It can take hours to reconfigure the engines."

Parn sighed. "Okay, I'll talk to him about his attitude and remind him he's supposed to give you a wide berth."

"Thanks."

Next he tracked down Mehany, who complained that Saicy was spending too much time with Urgot.

"Do you think he's forcing her somehow?"

"Yeah, I think that! He's done something."

"Have you talked to her? What has she said?"

Mehany looked away. "She says it's by choice. She says she wants to be with him." She shook her head. "But it doesn't feel right. Every time I ask about it, she gets weird. She's hiding something."

"Okay, I'll talk to her alone and see what she says. But," he touched her arm to make sure she was listening, "if I don't have any evidence that there's something going on, I can't act. If she won't tell me anything, you'll have to find some way to get something I can act on. Okay?"

Mehany grunted. "Yeah, fine. But something's wrong, believe me."

Parn next tracked Saicy down. She was in her cabin, sprawled on her couch in baggy clothes, going over pictures of herself and Ana working with the mecha. "Oh, hey, Parn, good of you to show up. Finish playing with the pepper?"

"I'm between harvesting shifts. Mehany said she was worried about you."

"She told me that, too. No worries. I'm fine."

"Are you? You don't sound like you're doing that well."

Saicy sighed and dismissed the image projection from her robot. She gave him an irritated look.

"Mehany said that you've been spending a lot of time with Urgot lately."

"Yeah. Nothing wrong with that, right?"

"You're right. It's your choice. I'm just surprised. Considering that last time we talked about it, you'd designed a robot just to keep him away from you."

"A girl can change her mind, can't she?"

"I just want to make sure that's what's happening here. Not you being forced to do things you don't want to."

Saicy's face brightened momentarily. "Trust me: Urgot can't make me do anything I don't want to do."

Parn found Urgot on the bridge, slouching and playing a digital game. "Hm, Captain," he grunted.

"Urgot, it's come to my attention that you accosted Birque and demanded that he reconfigure the engines for launch."

Urgot didn't turn from his screen. "Of course.

It's standard operating procedure. Ripe star pepper trees are explosive. We have to be ready to go if it looks like they might explode."

"But I told you to stay away from him. You should've come to me with that request."

"I might have." Urgot sat up and turned around to face Parn. "If you'd been here. Since you weren't here, I took the initiative."

"Don't expect a commendation from me." Parn tried to put as much authority into his voice as he could manage. "Even during my shift, I'm reachable. I received several communications from the ship while I was harvesting. But none of them were from you. In the future, Urgot, you need to try to contact me first, not act on your own."

"Yes . . . sir."

When Parn left the bridge, he wasn't sure what to do or think about his interviews with the crew. He had thought that once they had found the pepper, once it was getting loaded onto the ship, everything would be fine. Everyone would be looking forward to getting the cargo back to Xythas and collecting their money. But it seemed like things had gotten so much worse since they'd learned the pepper was here, and he didn't know why.

Then he realized that it had been a long time since he'd spoken with Mamillo. He'd hardly seen the doctor since before they landed. So he decided to check in at the infirmary.

When he entered the door, he gasped. There were Mamillo's plants, grown into a fantastic array of multicolored stems, leaves, tendrils, and flowers. It must be the features from at least a dozen different species grown into each plant. "Wow!" he said, not really expecting an answer.

But Mamillo said, "Thanks," from behind the screen of vines. "I think they've worked out pretty well, so far."

Parn came around the screen and saw Mamillo eating at a small table. "You take your meals in here, too, even when there're no patients?"

"Yes. I think the best way to survive a star voyage is always be exactly where and when you're needed. And when you're not needed, you should be alone."

"So, you're worried about surviving?"

"Me? No." One of Mamillo's laid back, disarming grins split his badly scarred face.

"What have you heard?"

"More than you'd think."

"So, what's going on?"

"I've never seen one before, but I think what's going on is mutiny."

Parn wandered out of the infirmary in a daze. How could he handle a mutiny? He needed time. And distance. Time he had, he realized. A mutiny couldn't be about anything but money. And that meant pepper. Right now, they had less than half of one hold of pepper. If Urgot was hoping to do better by reducing the number of shares, he would need more than that to make it worth his while. A mutiny now meant less money than he'd get if he just let the harvesting continue and then took his regular share. So he'd wait, let the harvesting continue. And, Parn decided, the harvesting would take place at a snail's pace.

In the hold, Parn saw Mehany. She looked like she was getting ready to head out on a harvesting trip. The spiderbot was fully prepped to go, and she was getting ready to climb on. He called to her, and she froze halfway up.

He hurried over to her. "What's the state of the free-ranging spiderbots?"

"Uh," she said, and her eyes unfocused. She did a few vague gestures and said, "Two are out. One of them has a full load and is getting ready to come back. The other is about three-quarters."

"Recall them both. And disable the independent harvesting mode for all the bots."

"What?" Mehany was crestfallen. "Don't tell me you're going to insist on us doing all of the harvesting? It'll take forever to fill these holds!"

"I dunno if I'm gonna insist on all of it. But I'm not sure I'm happy with their lots. I found some inhomogeneities. A bundle with grades A2 and A3 mixed."

Mehany snorted. "As if I've never done that! Hell, I bet even you've done that a few times."

"Maybe. But I think we need to revisit their autonomous routines before we can send them out again."

"Really?"

"You said it was a factory setting. I don't trust it. Remember what trouble we had when Saicy trusted the factory installed security on her robots? Let's disable this setting until we can sit down together."

"Are you gonna make time for that?"

"Yeah, I will. Soon. But, in the meantime, do

you think Saicy has the skills to reactivate the independent mode?"

"The skills, yeah. She's kind of a whiz at robotics. But she doesn't have the permissions. Should I give them to her?"

When Mehany mentioned permissions, Parn's heart skipped. "No, no. She doesn't need them. I'll sit down with you to review the modes." He gestured for Mehany to follow him. "In scouting around, Ana said she saw some dangerous animals. I think you should carry a sidearm."

They took the elevator to the infirmary deck. It also held the weapons locker. Parn took a deep breath before he accessed it. Then he breathed a sigh of relief. He could still access it. He took a pistol out and keyed it to Mehany. Then he took a second, third, and fourth one out. He keyed them to himself, Ana, and Birque. He thought about keying one to Mamillo, then decided he couldn't do that to the man. Mamillo would rather die than fire a gun, and not giving him one meant that he wouldn't find himself in a position where he might have to threaten with it, or accidentally shoot it.

As they took the elevator down to the engineering deck, Parn couldn't help but smile at his good fortune. Saicy could have cut him off from the weapons' locker. If she were fully invested in the mutiny, she would've done that already. That meant she was still undecided. And if Saicy wasn't committed, there was essentially no mutiny, yet. Just Urgot and his craftiness. And maybe Seldon. He checked the corer's activity log and was disappointed to see that the man hadn't been out harvesting. What was he doing?

Although Saicy might not be involved in a mutiny, something was definitely going on with her. It seemed that she was drifting more and more into Urgot's orbit. If she turned, that would be all Urgot would need. As owner and charter of the vessel, she could give him the permissions he needed to launch. With the engines in launch configuration, and Ana's Rho Space course laid in, Urgot had all he needed to launch and return home with the full load of pepper, and only two ways to split it.

Birque was attentively watching over the engines. He was monitoring their momentary mixes. Parn couldn't understand how the man could spend so much time looking at atomic collisions and not get bored. Parn held the gun out to him, handle first. "Ana saw some dangerous wildlife outside. I thought you should have a sidearm for safety," Parn said.

Birque scoffed. "Like I'm ever going to be outside."

"Just in case. It's better to be safe."

Birque smiled and shook his head. "Whatever you say, cap'n." He put the sidearm in the empty holster on his belt.

In the elevator, Parn called Ana and told her to meet him in the lower cargo bay, where the mecha was stored. He fingered the pistol he had authorized for her.

Mehany nodded toward it. "I notice you didn't issue a sidearm for Urgot."

Parn shrugged. "I didn't think of it. I got one for you because you were there when I thought of it. And I definitely want Ana to be safe."

"But Birque?"

Parn shrugged again. "I dunno. The guy just seems helpless. It seems like he needed it."

"Ha! I don't think that pistol will do him any good. What he really needs is a spine."

Parn grimaced. She was probably right.

In the lower bay, they met Ana. Parn gave her

the pistol. She held it tenderly in her hand, far out from her body. She looked at him quizzically.

"For safety. When you're outside."

"But I'm never outside without the mecha. What good would a pistol do me, then?"

"Maybe not a lot. But we're going to get out of the mecha today."

"What do you mean?"

"We're going to go to that village you found. We're going to talk to those people."

She smiled. "Really?"

Parn nodded.

Mehany shifted uncomfortably. Parn looked at her.

"And me? What am I going to do?"

Parn put his hand on her shoulder. "I think you should go harvest. I'm sorry I kept you so long. You can keep taking short shifts if you want."

Mehany snorted. "With the independent spiderbots disabled, I don't want to. I want to fill those holds and get out of here."

Parn nodded. Mehany got back in the elevator and headed away.

Part of Parn wanted that, too. But part of him was afraid of what would happen when those holds got full enough. He needed to find a solution before that happened.

Ana knew how to get the mecha down and run it through its checks, making sure all the batteries were fully charged and subsidiary power systems were ready if necessary, including the catalyst reservoir that could turn many common atmospheric gasses into fuel if necessary. As she started the checks, Parn said, "Hold on, I'll be right back."

Parn found Seldon in the rec room. He was watching a video. Parn called to him, and he waved absently, but didn't lift his eyes. Parn walked up close and stood over the chair where the other corer sprawled lazily. "I've been checking the logs and it seems you haven't been going out on very many harvesting shifts."

Seldon scoffed, but didn't look up from his video screen. "Why should I? I got a tiny share. Mehany got a share ten times as big as me—I think that means she oughta harvest ten times as much."

Parn pointed angrily at him. "That's not the way it works, and you know it. If you doubt me, check your contract. You want to get any share, you have to harvest."

Seldon looked away from his screen now. He

saw Parn's pointed finger and his face got really angry. "That's not fucking fair!"

Parn's pointed finger rolled into his fist. "You thought it was fair when you agreed to it."

Seldon stood up. "I didn't know you were cheating me."

"I'm not cheating you—you said yourself this is the largest share you've ever gotten. And if you just get off your ass and go harvest, you will make more money on this trip than on any you've been on before."

Seldon's hands also formed into fists. His eyes hardened. His jaw set.

"Another great way to lose your share is to start a fight on the ship."

Seldon groaned and turned away.

Parn looked at Seldon's back. Then he closed his eyes and took a breath. He drew on a piece of wisdom Vigar had told him. "Look, it's best not to think about the shares or the money or what's fair when you're harvesting. Just focus on the harvesting. Don't do it because you get paid, do it because you're a corer. It's what you are and it's what you do."

"That's easy for you to say—you've got a huge share."

Parn felt his blood rise, but he made himself take a breath before he spoke. "I think if you look at your contract, you'll see that you can actually make more than your shares. There are bonuses to be considered. Check your contract and see what you can do that I might give you a bonus for." He didn't wait for a reply but walked past Seldon out of the room.

When Parn got back to the ground, the mecha was ready. It was time for Parn to climb onto the back. Inside, there was only room for one person, and they needed their space to operate properly. But on the back there were handholds and footholds for three passengers. Parn took the center spot, which seemed to be the most secure, and even had a crash web to hold him tight against the metal skin of the mecha.

Parn initially wanted to do without the crash web, but Ana assured him that attempting it would lead to him either being thrown to his death or cracking his skull against the side of the mecha. And he quickly learned that she was right. It was a rough ride as the mecha took its long, loping strides across the susurrating green plains.

The grass was tall and wet, and the air was soon redolent with the smell of broken and seared stalks. Parn was afraid he was going to get seared, too. He could feel the heat of the mecha's actuators through the soles of his shoes. Intermittent blasts of heat also came from a vent at the back of the mecha's head.

Over the trip, Parn composed a long, scathing review of the accommodations for passengers on the back of the mecha, then deleted it when he realized this passenger area was intended only for emergencies. And it would serve in that situation. If he were badly wounded and needed to get back to the ship, strapping him on here would keep him reasonably safe. If they took the time to bind any abdominal wounds, because otherwise he was pretty sure his intestines would all be shaken out.

Then the mecha reached its destination. It stopped dead still, the grass stalks sizzling and popping where they touched the fully open radiant fins. Ana released the crash web, and Parn carefully stepped down, not needing the warning labels to tell him where the hot surfaces were—he could feel the heat through his clothes.

Once he had reached the ground, he looked around. This was clearly not the first time Ana had been to the area. Another clearing marked by the crushed, seared, and wilted grass stalks was visible across what seemed to be a well-trod path. The path had not been made by Ana. It was ancient, worn not just through the grass, but as a deep furrow in the earth itself. It was evidently a footpath, marked by what seemed to be hooves, with no sign of wheels or treads. It trailed back the way they had come, but led up a slight rise.

Parn was startled by a sound from behind him. It was Ana closing the front hatch on the mecha. She smiled at Parn, then looked back at the mecha. In a moment, it said, "Sentinel mode engaged."

Ana said, "In sentinel mode it will defend itself and come to our rescue if anything goes wrong. We can call for help, or if it senses trouble, it will retrieve us. Here."

A message notification appeared in the upper left of Parn's vision. He glanced at it. The message was asking permission to monitor his system using his native computer. Parn granted permission.

"Good," Ana said. "Now it'll rescue you, too."

"Are you expecting any trouble?"

"I haven't had any signs that there would be. But . . . you never know."

Parn nodded, then gestured for Ana to lead. She took the path, which sloped further up to what had once been a low, wide hill, but had been hollowed out to create a bowl. On one side of the entrance to the bowl, a watchman stood in a tower. The watchman was bipedal and had a pair of arms. They wore simple clothes: a loose tunic, loose pants, and a large sun hat that obscured their features. A companion tower had been allowed to fall into disrepair. As he approached the entrance, Parn noticed several other signs of fortification that had been allowed to atrophy: a fringing wall made of stone and wood, a gate to secure the entrance of the bowl.

Ana gestured at the watchman. The guard didn't raise a weapon or call a challenge as Ana walked past. From what Parn could see, the watchman didn't seem to have any weapons at all. Several berm houses had been built into the sides of the bowl. Most of them had tall, narrow doors, but one had an open front, revealing a forge and bellows, implements of metalworking as well as many products of the craft, and walls lined with baked brick. A large bonfire burned in the center of the bowl, contained in a well-built fire circle of blackened stone. Between the bonfire and the home entrances, the residents of the town sat or stood frozen, watching Ana and Parn as they approached. They had stopped mid-activity, except for some of the children who had obviously dropped their playthings and run for shelter behind their parents.

Parn could now see the people clearly. Their hands and faces were reptilian, covered by fine scales. The rest of their bodies—or at least what was visible of them—was covered with a soft down. Their clothes were mostly linen, colored brown, black, or earthy red, but there were also furs and skins evident, ranging from heavy shawls and cloaks to fine hats and decorative neckwear. They wore no visible shoes as their three-toed feet had sturdy hooves.

Ana said to Parn, "Last time I was here, I didn't have a translator installed on my computer, but I did record a lot of their language, then fed it into the translator back at the ship. Now we'll see how it worked."

Parn could hear Ana whispering to the computer. "Hello, again, friends. I am happy to return to your village and resume our friendship. I bring a gift—small lamps that can light a home without burning oil or torches." There was a strange chuffing sound from several of the people, especially the little ones. It sounded like they had all suddenly gotten very sick and were coughing.

One of the creatures came out of its door. It walked toward Ana with confidence and speed that concerned Parn, but Ana seemed untroubled. It made a gesture with its raised hand and said something. The chuffing broke out again, affecting more of the people and lasting longer. The translator said, "Welcome again, friend Atha."

Ana performed some adjustments, then said, "I am happy to be here. Shall we go inside and see how well the lamps work?"

The standing person made a brief, unconscious jerk, then calmed themselves and gestured to the door they had emerged from. Ana went to the doorway, but when Parn started to follow, the person gestured to stop him. Ana turned around and said, "This is Parn. He is my mate." Then Ana introduced him. "Parn, this is Kalakak, or anyway, that's what I call him."

Kalakak made a permissive gesture. He also spoke, and Parn thought he heard his name, but he couldn't be sure. Inside, there were two others of the creatures who stood with their backs against the earthen walls.

Ana had arranged the lamps on a low table that occupied much of the interior. "Here are the lamps I brought," she said.

Kalakak began to weave his head from side to side in an agitated fashion. Then he spoke. The translator said, "No, please, let me show you my lamp."

"No, you don't understand. I brought these so you wouldn't have to burn your lamp, so you could save your oil."

Now not just Kalakak, but the other two creatures began to move their heads in agitation. The leader gestured to them in a way that slowed their motions, but didn't stop them.

Then he turned and crouched down beside the table, his legs disjointing with a soft popping sound, then splaying out beside him in a way that made Parn cringe. He began speaking in a slow, steady way that seemed designed to allow them to follow, but didn't give them an opportunity to interrupt.

"Friend Ana," the translator interpreted, "you are a stranger and may not understand our ways, so let me explain to you what you are doing.

"Long ago, my people were wicked. They did not trust strangers and hoarded the light in their homes. They would not share with travelers unless they were paid generously. God saw our wickedness and warned us that if we did not share, we would suffer. But people did not repent.

"So God allowed the fields of the Ksut to grow fertile," the creature gestured in the direction of the star pepper grove, "and their empire grew strong, so strong that they came to us and demanded the light from our homes. We did not yield to the power of God, but built walls to protect our wickedness. For many years, we defended our homes and their light, but the empire of the Ksut grew too strong, and it broke our walls and stole our light, killing many of our people and taking many more as slaves.

"Then God showed us what happens to hoarders of light." The creature raised his right hand into the air, then chopped the air with it as he spoke. "Lights fell from the sky, bright lights that hit the fields and farms and cities of the Ksut. They suffered terribly, but the worst was to come. Their fields began to die, and as their food dwindled, so did their empire." He let his hand fall flat on the table.

"Some of them came to us, begging that we take them in. We had seen the vengeance of God, so we knew that the way of righteousness was to open our doors and let them into the light." He opened his arms out broadly. "So, you see, a stranger coming into my home bearing light is at least an insult to my hospitality and a temptation to hoard my light, and, at worst, an omen of doom to come. So, please, put away your lamps and let me show you mine."

Ana did as requested, and Kalakak lit his oil lamp. It cast a flickering, yellow light that Parn found warm and comforting, albeit a bit dimmer than he'd like. With the yellow lamps, the dirt walls of the home disappeared into blackness, and Parn got a feeling that the walls were now crawling with vermin.

Ana said, "Is that why you are so open? Why your city has no defenses?"

"Hospitality is our defense. As long as we honor His command, God will protect us."

"You have no fear, then, not even of opening your city to people as strange as us?"

Kalakak leaned forward into the light. "It is because our city is open that we have no fear. And it is especially important to welcome strange persons as yourself—God tests us."

"If that is the test, then you have passed, my friend."

The creatures made their soft chuffing sound again, and it made Parn uncomfortable. Kalakak said, "I do not know who taught your interpreter how to speak, but they did a very bad job."

"What do you mean?" Ana asked.

"You say 'friend' when you mean 'friend.' But 'friend' means a furry creature that makes bowers in the grass."

"Oh. I see." There was a pause. Ana said, "I want to teach my interpreter better. Say the two different words."

Kalakak said the words. They sounded the same

to Parn, and the interpreter said they both meant friend.

"Now say the one that means someone you like. Say it three times."

Kalakak did.

"Now say the furry creature three times."

Parn thought he might have been able to tell the difference, but he couldn't be sure. The translator could tell the difference, though, now saying "furry creature," each time the leader spoke.

"Okay," Ana said. "Now, tell me, friend, if this is better."

Kalakak opened his mouth and let his tongue loll out. It made a few sounds, then the translator said, "Much better."

Parn said, "Ask him if he knows the star pepper trees are still dangerous."

Kalakak replied, "They are not dangerous. They are our protectors. They grow tall to show the might of God and keep all invaders away. Instead, traders and travelers come to visit us, and we welcome them all." Then he led the conversation on to food, offering various fruits and prepared dishes to try, which Ana did.

Parn sniffed everything suspiciously. He tried a

few things but found them universally tart. Even the bread was sour. His mind would sometimes wander back to the question of the mutiny, then forward to the time when these people would be faced with the destruction of their world due to the star pepper.

He got a signal on his com from Urgot, and he wanted to ignore it, but then he was afraid of what the pilot might try to do on his own. Parn leaned over to Ana, "There's a signal from the ship. I need to answer it. Can you excuse me politely?"

Ana nodded, then put her hand on his arm to hold him in place while she asked for him to be excused. After some formalities, she lifted her hand and nodded to him.

Parn nodded at the aliens, then left the cave. Outside, he called the ship, with his signal being relayed from the mecha.

"Parn," Urgot's voice was angry, "I just found out that you issued most of the crew sidearms."

"Yeah, uh, Ana said she saw some dangerous local animals, so I wanted people to be safe."

"Why didn't you issue one to me? Don't you want me to be safe?"

"Think of it as incentive to stay on the ship.

You're our only liftoff pilot, so it's better if you stay on the ship."

"Birque's our only engineer. You gave him a pistol. You want him wandering all over?" Parn could hear his sneer over the com.

"Well, Urgot, since you had him put the engines in launch mode already, he's not strictly necessary for launch, is he?"

Although Parn paused, Urgot didn't respond.

"So, anyway," Parn continued, "just sit tight and don't worry about the sidearms."

"Sure. Anything you say . . . captain." Then he signed off.

When Parn went back inside, Ana looked at him, concerned. Parn just shook his head to show he didn't want to talk about it.

It was dark outside by the time they took their leave from Kalakak. Outside the village, Parn said, "Should we tell them what's going to happen with the star pepper trees?"

"Do you think they'd believe us? You heard how they feel about the trees—they're a gift from god."

"I think we should still warn them. Did you

know that almost all harvesting expeditions set off the pepper trees?"

"No."

"It's usually a fire in one of the partially harvested trees that starts it. It's small and goes unnoticed. But it smolders and then blazes and then the grove explodes. That's why we almost never go back to pepper planets we've already harvested."

Before climbing up into the mecha, Ana looked back at the village. She asked, "As close as they are to the trees, what are their chances?"

Parn sighed and also looked back at the village, with the blazing central fire he had first spotted while harvesting. "At this range—it's almost certain they'd be destroyed. I've been a on a few expeditions where we got to pepper planets after the explosions. We do scientific survey work to keep the trip from being a complete waste."

He gestured out at the darkness. "This entire continent will be wiped out. The firestorm and the pollution will then wipe out most of the life on the planet. Some biospheres recover. Most don't."

"So what's the point of telling them? They can't move far enough away to get safe."

Parn shrugged. "I don't like the thought that

they're doomed and we're not telling them. I want to be honest with them." Parn didn't like the thought that these kind, hospitable people would soon be another sacrifice to the pepper trade. The least he could do is make sure they weren't ignorant sacrifices.

"Honest before we kill them?"

"We're not killing them. And it's possible we won't set off the trees. We're a small expedition. Mehany and I are careful harvesters."

"But what about the robots?"

Parn shrugged. "I dunno. Maybe that's another reason why the company never used the robots as independent harvesters. But it doesn't really make a difference. As mature as these trees are, it's only a matter of time before they go off naturally. Lightning. A drifting spark from these people's fire that contacts with the flammable outgassing from the trees. It's going to happen."

Ana stopped. She grabbed Parn's arm. "There's no point to telling them. But maybe we can move them?"

"Now that would be pointless. Worse—it'd be cruel. Say we move them to the other side of the world. Then they don't die in the explosion, but they'll choke on the toxic gasses or starve when all the plants and animals die off. There's no place on the planet where they'd be safe."

"I didn't say on the planet. Look!" she pointed up at a bright, blue-green star. It didn't twinkle like the other stars—it shone with a steady, colorful light. "Remember that I said there were two likely pepper planets in this system? There's a good chance that other planet is also habitable, and we can take them there!"

Parn hugged her. He felt a tremendous relief. "Ana, you're brilliant! That would be worth checking out. Our probe is still in orbit here—it should be able to look at the other planet to check out the atmosphere. Then we can move the people over there. Our holds are big enough to accommodate their entire community." Parn frowned. "But we'd have to convince them to go."

"I'm not too worried about them. I think we can manipulate the signs of their faith to convince them that their god wants them to go.

Parn thought about it. It seemed like the right thing to do. It's what he wanted to do. More importantly, it seemed like what Vigar would do, and what he'd want Parn to do. But it wasn't what Astreyan would do. Parn felt that this was the opportunity to prove he was Vigar's true successor, and the rightful heir to this pepper planet. Then he shook his head. "But it will involve postponing the harvesting operations, removing the pepper from the hold, and putting all the returns at risk. Do you think we can convince Saicy? Or Urgot?"

Ana smiled and ran her finger along the epaulet of his uniform. "Well, are you the captain, or aren't you?"

Parn realized he couldn't truly answer that question.

CHAPTER 20

Riding the mecha in the dark was somehow even more terrifying. When the machine crouched down at the ship, Parn could barely wait for the safety net to be released. He climbed down clumsily, his pounding heartbeats surging in his temples. Then he accidentally touched one of the cooling fins, and his flesh sizzled. He cursed and fell away, landing on the soft earth. He lay still with his eyes closed. He was trying to find some measure of calm. After all, he wasn't badly hurt.

He opened his eyes, and there was Urgot, crouched over him. He did not look happy. "Parn, why have you stopped sending out the spiderbots to harvest? That's going to slow us down."

Parn scooted along the ground away from Urgot. Then he sat up. "If you're worried about the time, we can go right now. Because if we fill our holds with spiderbot-harvested pepper, I guarantee you we'll earn less than we will for what's already in our hold."

"What?"

Parn stood up, dusting himself off. "I suppose you'll probably still earn more than you would with typical shares on a commercial voyage. But I thought you wanted to be rich."

"Stop, just tell me what you're talking about."

Parn sighed. "Obviously, you're not a corer. Look, how do you think we get paid for our cargo?"

"Someone buys it."

"Right," Parn said, and patted Urgot on the shoulder. "But how do they know how much to pay us?"

"By how much pepper we have?"

"Partly, but it's not just the weight. It's also the grade. Not only that, but the homogeneity of the grades. They only pay grade A price if a lot is pure grade A. If it's mixed with grade B, they only pay grade B price for the whole lot. And if there are too many mixed-grade lots, the entire cargo gets down-graded, and that will really cost us."

Urgot shook his head and held out his hands, questioning.

Parn sighed again and walked past Urgot, not looking back as he talked. "The bots were mixing the lots too much, and they were harvesting too much of the pepper. They were really going to cost us. So, until we have them recalibrated, only humans will harvest star pepper. That's my order."

Parn climbed up the steps into the ship. About halfway up he stopped and looked back down at Urgot, who had turned his eyes to Ana. Urgot made a silent, questioning gesture. Ana shrugged and went back to working on the mecha. Parn went into the ship. He wanted to be ready to head out for coring when Mehany got back.

Parn looked over Mehany's load. "These look great. Nicely homogenous lots. The way only a human can do it."

She looked at him and sighed. As she did, her entire frame sank in exhaustion to the bench behind her. She was just half out of her coring suit, her skin sweaty and red in most places, except where contact with the suit had pressed it white. "That's bullshit and you know it. I don't have energy for that right now. Can you tell me what's going on with Urgot or not?"

Parn looked away, then looked back. "No, not yet. But here's what I want you to do about the spiderbots. Break them all down except for the one I'm going to take. Examine their harvesting routine and try to figure out if that's something we can tweak.

"Then explore the guard mode to see what kind of parameters we can put on that. We may need them. And while you're at it, make sure you lock Saicy out of them, if you can."

Mehany growled. Then she said, "Can I at least get some sleep first?"

Parn nodded. Mehany grunted and got to her feet, unzipping her suit. She exchanged a wave with Parn as he turned to his locker, then started trying to wiggle out of her suit.

Parn took off the shirt of his captain uniform, folded it carefully, and put it in his locker. He found himself staring at it, wishing he'd never put it on. When he agreed to take the navigation crystal from Vigar, he had no idea he'd end up in a situation like this. He just wished he knew what to do.

Well, what to do now was get ready for coring.

He stripped out of the rest of his uniform, then got into the cooling undergarments designed to be worn under his suit. He heard the shower go on and glanced up to see Mehany slouched under the water, barely holding herself upright.

He was delighted to have the spiderbot carry him out and away from the ship. The robot was much slower than the mecha, and much more comfortable for him, even though he was much higher in the air. The spiderbot took him to the tree he had been working on. He had just finished a chamber, so he had to cut into a new one.

Although he tried to keep himself thinking about the mutiny and the cave people who would need to be saved, he got lost in the coring. His mind would focus on the charcoal-grey putty, always on the lookout for slight variations in color or firmness of the material that would indicate changes in grade. Keeping the lots as uniform as possible, both in quality and size, was an engrossing task for him. Hand and eye and mind, maintaining the steady rhythm of cutting a kilo every two seconds or so, took him away from his personal worries. It was hard to focus on the conflicts he was facing when peace was so readily at hand.

It was early morning when he paused to eat outside the tree. Although there was a hint of light on the horizon, the sky and the land were black. As he chewed his protein bar, he looked out over the plains to see the cave people's fire. There it was, bright and jovial. He wondered if they kept it burning brightly all night or if they had recently fired it up for their morning needs. Then he panned his vision toward the ship.

His eyes stopped on a spar of bright red light jutting up into the night sky. A fire in the stage one trees. That fire would rapidly spread through the stage one trees, then reach the stage two trees, which wouldn't just burn, they'd explode. Parn had hoped to string Urgot along for several tendays, even a pentad, but now he had only hours before the entire grove would explode.

Parn ordered the spiderbot to take him to the ship. As it bore him along with its partial load of star pepper, the light of dawn crept over the land. Although it overtook the fire raging in the trees, that small fire seemed to be spreading so much more alarmingly fast. He lost sight of it for a while, but when he reached the ship, he could see it was close, and getting closer. He ordered the spiderbot to place its cargo in the hold, then shed his protective suit outside. At this point, it didn't seem worth it to collect the dregs from his suit, and he wouldn't need it anymore.

Wearing just his cooling underwear, he ran into the ship. He stopped at the locker room just long enough to grab his sidearm, the captain's shirt, and his hat. He didn't feel he had time to put the uniform on, but he thought some visible reminder of rank might help. He fastened the weapons belt and hat on before he headed out but slipped the shirt on as he ran. It hung loose around him as he ran, letting the air evaporate the cold sweat off his chest.

He ran into Mehany first. She had been crying, but she looked relieved to see him.

"Did you see the fire?"

She nodded. "It was Birque. I . . . I mean, Urgot killed Birque. And that started the fire."

"Where's Ana?"

Mehany looked like she might start crying again. "She went out to the village. First thing this morning. We didn't know about the fire then."

"Did you call her back?"

She shook her head. "Urgot's cut off communication. We can't get a hold of her."

"It doesn't matter." Urgot said.

Parn spun around and saw the pilot at the other end of the hall. He was holding Saicy in front of him, a gun pointed at her. Seldon stood behind, his face firm and unreadable.

"We're going to leave all of you here. As you said, I want to get rich off this expedition, and I can't do that splitting this short cargo among all of us. But split fewer ways, it makes a tidy profit."

Parn wanted to draw his pistol, but with Saicy at risk, he didn't dare. Instead, he looked at her and said, "You gave him a pistol?"

Saicy was remarkably calm when she said, "I didn't think he'd use it. Especially not at a setting powerful enough to start a fire like that!"

Parn said with disgust, "Crew knows nothing about the pepper."

Urgot yelled, "I know enough to make a fortune on it. Which is more than enough, and, it turns out, more than you!"

Parn realized and said, "You won't shoot her, you need her to claim the pepper!"

As Parn was drawing his pistol, Urgot said, "But I don't need you!" He began firing. Parn and Mehany ran for cover. They ran down the side passage that led to the locker room. Parn managed to get to cover, but Mehany cried out in pain as she got hit.

In the locker room, Mehany looked at her wound. Parn flinched as she pulled aside her blouse to reveal the large, blackened area where the molten projectile had hit. Urgot had obviously dialed down the setting from when he killed Birque, but it was still a dangerous hit. And it meant his gun was set high enough to seriously damage the ship if there were too much loose firing going on.

Parn also looked around for any cover the locker room might afford. There wasn't much. The benches were no good. The banks of lockers provided only moderate cover from the angle of the door, and if Urgot maneuvered through the room, they'd be no cover at all. The corers could duck into the showers, but then they'd be trapped.

"I think we've got to keep withdrawing," Parn said.

"Or you could just shoot the fucker," Mehany growled back.

"I can't. I'd probably hit Saicy. He's using her as a shield."

"So what? She's obviously thrown in with him. Good riddance to her."

"Maybe, but we need her as much as Urgot does. She's the true owner of the ship, and it won't lift off without her."

Mehany grumbled but followed Parn as they crossed the locker room. "The problem with this plan," she said, "is that there's no place to go from here but outside. Once we're out there, he can just take off without us."

"No, we can climb up the entry to the cargo hold. If we're lucky, the spiderbot's transmitter will let us get in touch with Ana. Or, at least, we'll be with the pepper. Hopefully, even he isn't stupid enough to fire at us in a hold full of pepper."

Parn rushed Mehany ahead of him. Looking over his shoulder, he saw Saicy being pushed into the locker room just as it vanished around the corner.

Outside, Parn encouraged Mehany to climb the ladder to the hold. She tried, but winced. "I can't," she said.

Parn grimaced. He gestured down the ramp. "Get down and out of the way. Find cover. I'll try to get inside and deal with him from there. "

She nodded and started to head down the ramp. Parn grabbed the ladder and started up toward the open hatch. He hadn't gotten nearly as far as he'd hoped by the time Urgot and Seldon came out. Parn glanced down at Urgot. He saw and heard he was turning up the power on his pistol. Parn stopped climbing and focused on Urgot as he took aim. As the pilot's eyes narrowed, Parn threw himself from the ladder. He heard the shot and saw the fiery bolt pass by. He could even feel the heat of it in the palms of his hands. The air whistling by Parn's ears distorted the sound of Urgot's cursing. Then Parn hit the ground flat on his back.

The ground was soft, but the impact knocked the wind out of Parn, and for a moment, all he could do was struggle to breathe. When he could focus again, he was looking up at Urgot aiming the pistol down at him. Mehany was yelling from nearby. He had hoped that she would be safely in cover by now. Yelling at Urgot wasn't going to do any good. As soon as he finished killing Parn, he'd turn the gun on her. Parn sighed, knowing they'd both soon be dead.

But instead of the whoosh of the pistol, Parn

heard the rat-tat-tat of a machine-gun. Armor-piercing bullets swarmed around Urgot and Seldon. Several of them struck the ship and went right through the hull. One hit Seldon, blowing his torso apart. Blood splattered the hull and the body hit the ground between Parn and the landing gear.

Parn turned to see the source of the gunfire. The mecha was approaching at high speed. Although it wasn't firing, the gun was raised and ready. Urgot cowered and ran back toward the ship. Saicy poked her head out the door, then shouted, "Stand down!" Parn heard the mecha powering down. Saicy ran into the ship after Urgot.

Parn looked back over at the mecha. Ana was a pantomime of anger until the hatch opened to release her curses. "Sorry," she said, "I really wanted to get that sucker."

"That would've been great. But you saved me, anyway. I'm glad for that!"

Parn looked back at the ship. The hatch closed and the ramp retracted. Parn felt a strong hand grab his upper arm. He looked up at Mehany. He grabbed her arm. The big woman winced as she pulled Parn away from the ship to the tree line.

About halfway there, Parn managed to get to his feet. He staggered with Mehany into the forest.

Now all the hatches on the ship were closed. The engines were powering up. Parn looked at Ana, who yelled, "I'm gonna hunker down here." Parn nodded. Then she closed the mecha's hatch. Parn and Mehany turned and ran away from the ship. They didn't know how far they had to get to be clear of the launch blast. The clearing had been big enough for the tiny braking burn, but liftoff would likely destroy many of the closest trees.

As they heard the engine begin to release its growling thrust, they threw themselves into a small culvert. They felt the heat around them, but they could tell it wasn't dangerous. As the thrust receded, they stood up. The flames of the ship were disappearing against the bright midmorning sky.

Parn lowered his gaze and saw that the trees at the edge of the clearing were on fire. Soon, that fire would meet up with the one that was already burning, trapping them in the forest. "Let's get out of here," Parn said and gestured for the gap.

Mehany nodded and the two rushed through the underbrush for the forest edge. Once there, Parn looked to see how the mecha had fared. It seemed fine. Its pink armor was not even blackened, although the grass all around it had been crisped and was still burning in some places. Then the hatch opened, and Ana waved.

Parn and Mehany crossed the fiery field. As he got close to the mecha, he said, "Wow, the hull can really hold up in a pinch. But now we've got to leave it behind." He gestured at the middle of the star pepper grove. "I suggest we go that way. Then at least the end will be quick."

Ana shook her head. "No. We don't have to give it up at all. The command Saicy used is a short-term one. There are permanent ones, but she didn't want to do that. She wanted us to have the mecha."

"What good will it do us?" Mehany asked. "It's just a slower death, one way or the other."

"No," Parn said, scratching his chin. "It's a chance. We should take it."

Mehany groaned. "Parn, we've been to worlds after the star pepper launches. You know as well as I do that there won't be any breathable air and nothing to eat. Not for centuries."

"No, you're right." Parn looked up at the sky.

"Still, it's a chance. Does this have a transponder that you can turn on?" he asked Ana.

Ana looked at the control panel absently. "I can turn the transponder off. But it's on by default, I think. Should I turn it off when the systems come on?"

"No, let's leave it on."

Parn and Mehany sat down at the mecha's feet. They watched the fire burn in the stage one trees. After a while, the heat was starting to be too much. It was so uncomfortable that the unpleasant thought of getting up to move began to seem like the smart choice.

"How long until that thing turns on?" Parn asked.

"I don't know," Ana said. "I just know that the stand down command is temporary."

"Are you sure?" Mehany said. "If we don't really know that it's going to come on, I can think of many more comfortable places to wait for the end."

"Yeah, I'm sure. Saicy taught me all about this thing"

Mehany pounded the dirt. "And you still trust that ewe?"

"What reason would she have to lie to me then?"

"Who knows how long she's been conspiring with Urgot? I thought she was my friend when she was helping me work on the spiderbots. But maybe she was just trying to figure out how to work them so she could cut us out."

Parn stood up. "I don't think she was working with him that long. I think I could tell when it changed." He offered a hand to Mehany.

Mehany snorted. "Yeah, sure. Her titties got you so turned around I bet you can't believe she's working with him even now."

Parn was silent. Mehany and Ana both scoffed. Parn shrugged. He offered Mehany his hand again. She sighed and grabbed it with her uninjured arm. She winced as she stood up. "We're gonna go a little further from the fire to wait." He gestured toward the place where the clearing opened up into the plain of tall, green grass.

Before they got halfway to the opening, the mecha beeped. "Hey, it's on!" Ana yelled.

Mehany groaned and looked up at the sky. "I'm not walking back there."

"No need. I'll come to you." She closed the

hatch and in one quick leap the mecha was standing in front of the corers.

"Where to now?" Mehany asked.

"The village," Ana said.

"What village?" Then she nodded her head. "Oh, you mean the one with the indiginies?"

"Yes!" Ana turned to Parn. "The probe showed that the atmosphere on the other planet should be compatible with their physiology. We can transport them there safely."

"That's great!" Parn replied.

Mehany humphed. "Assuming Saicy comes back for us . . ."

Ana and Parn nodded reluctant agreement.

Mehany needed help getting up and Parn had to support her while Ana fastened the safety web around her. The whole time Parn was holding her, he was watching the fire spread. Thankfully, it seemed like the direction of fastest spread was away from the stage two trees. Still, the fire was probably creeping that direction, too. It was growing unbearably hot and the air was full of fumes. Stage one star pepper trees were similar to normal trees. They were woody with cellulose, but they were also full of aromatic compounds, so they smelled like particle board burning.

Then it was Parn's turn to climb up. He was practically an old pro by this time and could get himself fastened in, so Ana rushed back to the cockpit.

As the mecha powered up, Mehany looked at him, her eyes pleading. "Is this as bad as being carried by a spiderbot?"

Parn considered the lie, then said, "It's much worse."

"Suck."

Then the mecha was leaping across the land. They left the smell of fumes behind. After a few leaps, Parn felt a fine spray of warm liquid that stank of vomit. He couldn't hear Mehany's heaves, but when the mecha stopped, he could hear her sobs. She quickly choked them down. By the time Parn had let himself down and could see her, she was glowering and impatient. Only her puffy eyes and vomit-spattered shirt showed how hard the journey had been on her. Parn decided to wait for Ana before unfastening Mehany.

When Ana unfastened her, Mehany almost fell on top of Parn. He managed to cushion her descent, and she tried, too, although her legs were wobbly. She didn't crush Parn and she didn't end up on the ground, which seemed pretty miraculous good fortune given her condition.

"I can't believe I let you talk me into that," she said. "And for what? You think she's coming, but she's not coming."

Ana looked at Parn. "You think she's coming?"

"I do."

Ana put her hand on Parn's arm. "Saicy isn't coming back. She's left us for good."

"Then why did she only give the temporary pause command?"

Ana shrugged. "Maybe it's just the one that came out first. Maybe she didn't know how star pepper trees affect the planet and she thought we could survive better if we had the mecha."

Parn glared at Ana. "Look, if you don't trust me, trust Mamillo."

Mehany said, "I trust Mamillo, but I don't know what he's got to do with it."

"Do you think he would've sat back and let the ship lift off with him on it if it was going to be leaving us behind?"

Mehany said, "I think he might not have

known what was happening. It all went pretty fast."

"It seemed pretty fast to us, but not to Mamillo. When he doesn't have patients, he just sits and prunes his plants and thinks about what's happening on the ship. He knew about this mutiny before any of us. I bet he also figured out long ago what he was going to do about it. There's no way this took him by surprise."

Ana and Mehany just looked at Parn, incredulous.

Parn groaned. "Fine. Look, if we prepare for Saicy to come and she doesn't, then the worst we've done is find a diversion for our final hours. But if she does come and we haven't prepared, we'll have missed an opportunity to do some real good."

Mehany shrugged. Ana said, "Okay, I guess that's right."

Parn sighed. "Thank you. I really believe that she will come back, and in the meantime, we have to get ready." He looked at Ana. "You said you thought you could convince Kalakak's people to come with us?"

"I do. Let's give it a try." She reached into the cockpit of the mecha. Then she ordered it into sentry mode. She said, "I don't know exactly how they'll respond to this. We may be fighting for our lives until the trees explode."

"Or Saicy comes," Parn said.

Ana shrugged. They walked toward the village. When they could see the lightly armed sentry in the ruined tower, she ignited the flare. The zirconium-based flare burst into brightness. It was designed to be seen from orbit at any time of day, and the brightness of it turned the area around them a ghostly white, taking all the vibrancy that natural sunlight gave to the plants and rocks. The sentry blinked, then shielded his eyes and retreated from the tower in fear.

Ana strode boldly up the path into the village. She stood at the gate, holding the flare high. People gasped. Children cried. Fear and trembling paralyzed the village.

Ana spoke loudly. Her voice had a deep bass tone that surprised Parn, and he couldn't believe the commanding figure that her slender, waifish form presented. "Fear not, people of Kistik. God has seen your goodness. We came to test your hospitality, and you have proven yourselves worthy. But the rest of the world has not. It must be destroyed. So now the doom that came to Ksut will be used to burn the world pure with an all-consuming fire."

She threw the flare into the central bonfire. The effect of the shifting shadows as it tumbled end-over-end sent a new wave of fear through the assembled people. But when it landed in the bonfire and cast its light out from there, they all turned their eyes back to Ana.

"Kalakak," she called out. One of the people detached himself from his family and came forward. Parn couldn't tell if it was the leader, but Ana acknowledged him. He disjointed his legs and fell to the ground before her. "God has chosen to save your people, but they must be ready to travel. Tell them to gather all the food they can carry. Gather also all the seeds you would use in your planting, and all the fruits that you normally enjoy over the year. Anything that grows here will be destroyed and must be regrown in your new home. "

She put her hand on his shoulder. "Go now and tell your people to prepare. We must be ready to travel before the sun sets."

Kalakak nodded and stood. He started yelling instructions, presumably passing on Ana's orders.

The people were still terrified, but they slowly began to work. Even the children began to gather food after a short time of extra comfort.

"That was awesome!" Parn said.

"Yeah," Mehany said. Then she winced. "But who told you we had until sunset? We may not have that long."

Ana shrugged. "If we get killed before that, then they'll be in the midst of preparations, and they won't be aware of the deception."

Parn nodded. "Dying while working is not the worst way to go."

Mehany scoffed. "Ha! So you've given up on her, too?"

"No," Parn said, looking up at the sky. "I'm just saying. Besides, she may not know how little time we have, either. Her plans might not work out fast enough. And we'll die despite her best intentions."

Mehany laughed until the pain made her stop. Then she punched Parn hard enough to make him stagger. "You'll die with your faith intact, anyway." She grinned. Parn looked at the ground sheepishly.

As he watched the panicked chaos of Kalakak's people trying to assemble their belongings, he began to feel guilty. He wondered if his faith was indeed misplaced. Perhaps it was better to let the people spend their last hours in peaceful ignorance, unaware of the doom that approached. The sun moved across the sky and approached the western horizon. The sky grew hazy as the day progressed, and by late afternoon, the sun was becoming pale. The sky grew red, and between the setting sun and the firelight that was glowing to the north, the entire world became bathed in a deep blood tone.

And then Kalakak approached Ana. "My people are ready, emissary of God. You can bring the transport."

Ana looked at Parn. Parn shrugged and looked at the ground. He sighed. Ana punched him. Then she hugged him. As she let three sobs escape, Parn looked over her shoulder at the forest blazing in the north. Despite the driving wind, the fire would reach the stage two trees any time now, if they hadn't already.

Ana pulled herself away and looked Parn in the eyes, her hands still on his shoulders. He responded to her silent question with a nod. It was time to confess to Kalakak that no help was coming. She took a deep breath and squeezed his shoulders. She turned to the assembled people.

But before she could speak, the air around her brightened. Kalakak's people pointed to the sky and began to shout. Several of them fell to their knees.

Parn turned and looked up at the sky. Four bright blue lights stood out against the hazy, darkening sky. The spectrum of very hot fusion drives. As they approached, it was clear they were landing near the mecha. Far enough from the village to avoid damage, but close enough for easy access. Behind him, Ana was speaking to Kalakak's people. He didn't hear her words, but they brought exhortations from the gathered folk.

As it landed, Parn charged toward the ship. He approached as close as the heat would let him, edging forward, although it was clear the engines were still in liftoff configuration by the high heat they generated. When the ramp came down, it was practically at his feet. He ran up it. The door opened. Saicy stood in the doorway, her hips tilted, one fist on the upturned side. She made a flourishing gesture. "Anyone need a ride?" she called out, her voice so casual and lilting that the blazing death around them seemed to be on another planet, far away in space.

"Yes!" Parn shouted. "You certainly took your time!"

Saicy smiled. "I came as fast as I could. I had to wait until Urgot let his guard down. Then Mamillo could drug him and I could come back for you."

Mehany, who Parn didn't know was right behind him, said, "I didn't know you were a pilot!"

Saicy laughed, "Neither did Urgot. I find it's useful to keep some of my skills a secret. And when you look like this," she gestured to herself and did a little shimmy, "it's easy to get people to underestimate you."

They all laughed. Ana called from the foot of the ramp, "Can we start boarding?"

Saicy yelled back. "Yes! Have people leave their stuff at the foot of the ramp. I'll set up directional indicators to tell them where they should go. Mehany, can you get the spiderbots to carry the stuff into the top cargo bay?"

Mehany nodded, then pushed past Parn to get to the bots. Parn saw he couldn't get down the ramp, so he led the tide, directing people to the lowest cargo bay until Saicy had configured the indicators in the corridors. After a few minutes of this, Parn realized that he could communicate with the main computer to get the translator program that Ana used. After that, it went a little smoother. Still, the people didn't like being crowded into the cargo hold. He didn't have time to answer their questions. Whenever they complained, he replied with, "God will reward your sacrifice." That seemed to quiet them pretty well, so he repeated it often.

The biggest challenge was when the first cargo bay was full and he had to redirect them down the hallway and up a ladder to get to the next one. As the second cargo bay was filling, Parn went to scout out the third bay. The outside door was open, and the spiderbots were loading baskets and pots into it. Mehany was monitoring their efforts from the edge of the bay. Parn walked over to her, nodding a greeting and looking down. There were a few people on the ramp, but it was not a crush. He looked around for Ana, but didn't see her. He concluded she must be in the mecha, which was walking around at the foot of the ramp.

Then a bright light flashed on the horizon. Parn

looked. He couldn't see the light, but he heard the crack of thunder roll across the land and saw the shockwave roll over the grassland. A single fiery trail was climbing into the sky. "Smut!" Mehany said. She focused on the distance and must have been issuing commands to the spiderbots because they all began hurrying up to the bay, whether they had burdens or not.

Parn hailed Ana, "That was the first star pepper detonation. You need to get on board now!"

Ana said, "Not everyone's on, yet!"

"Tell them to hurry! I'll tell Saicy to raise the ramp and close the door. Anyone who isn't inside will have to be left behind. You need to get in here. Now, dammit, now!"

Ana said, "Okay," then began relaying his instructions to the people at the base of the ramp.

Parn called to Saicy, "That was the first explosion. They'll start coming more frequently. We need to be off the ground in minutes!"

"Understood." The claxon sounded and the ramp began to rise. People were pushing and rushing to get in.

The last spiderbots climbed in the upper cargo bay, then the mecha jumped and landed gingerly just inside the door, which began to close. Three bright flashes illuminated the mecha through the closing door, followed by overlapping thunders. Once Parn had gotten a glimpse of Ana's nervous face through the mecha's window, he went back down to direct people into the second cargo bay. It was full. Although he knew there was still room in the third bay above, he didn't dare direct them up there—he didn't want anyone on the ladder when the ship began to lift off. Instead, he urged them to sit along the hallways. When the hallways were full, he sent a message over the PA in their language to tell them to hunker down where they were.

The announcement had barely finished when the engines shook the ship and gravity began to increase. He let the thrust pull him down into a crouch, the best position he could manage with the crowding and without a crash couch.

Shortly after takeoff, the ship shook with turbulence. People screamed in terror as they were thrown around. An announcement came over the PA in the native language: "Fear not, for you are in the hands of God. The way is hard, and the chosen are few, but He safeguards your passage."

The cries quieted, replaced by the murmurings

of prayer. Parn smiled. Ana had really internalized their religious rhetoric. He patched into Saicy, "How are we doing?"

She spoke through gritted teeth. "Well, I've never taken off under fire, but I think we're going to make it." After a moment, she followed up with, "You weren't kidding about the destruction. The area we left is completed flattened. It looks like the entire world is on fire!"

After a while, the thrust cut off and they were in zero gravity. This created almost as much panic as the turbulence. A voice came over the PA in natives' language, and Parn's Tri-I translated it for him. "Your burdens may have been heavy, but now they are light. Relax and trust to the care of the Lord." Again, the screams quieted and were replaced by murmurs of prayer.

Parn climbed up the ladder to the bridge. Saicy welcomed him there. Parn said, "If this was your plan, why didn't you help us take care of Urgot before?"

Saicy said, "He didn't let his guard down until we were in space."

"Together, we could've gotten him before he lifted off."

"Yeah, but you wanted to leave the pepper behind. I didn't want to do that!"

"You would choose profit over people's lives?"

Saicy looked at him with a puzzled expression. "What are you talking about? You don't have to choose one or the other if you plan it right."

Parn groaned. "You came awfully damn close to sacrificing these people's lives for your profit!"

Saicy smiled. "if you're not cutting it close, you're not maximizing your potential." She gestured for Parn to come closer. He drifted within reach. She pulled him into a hug. "Don't worry. We're here. We're safe. All these people are safe. And we have a highly profitable load of star pepper in orbit, too. Not to mention a great story to sell."

Parn didn't struggle. He sighed and let the hug comfort him. Saicy's arms were strong, but her body was soft. After a while, Parn felt better. He decided to let his concerns go for now and focus on the fact that, no matter what else, she had come for them.

Parn broke away. "I'm going to reconfigure the engines for landing. We completely destroyed these people's old home, the least we can do is minimize the singe on their new one."

CHAPTER 21

Epilogue

The second potential planet also had star pepper trees on it, but they were much less mature. The seeds must have landed several hundred years later than on the other planet, so there were mature stage one trees, but the stage two trees were small and woody, without any pepper at all.

It also didn't seem to have any intelligent life. At least, when surveying the night side of the planet, there were no light sources that exceeded 800 lumens per square mile, other than wildfires. Saicy's assistant, Capella, said that this survey was essential for filling out the forms required under the Refugee Resettlement Regimen. Once they were satisfied that the new planet was free of indigenous intelligence, they happily skipped form 378-B and landed near the star pepper grove developing in the southern hemisphere.

After landing, Parn and Ana helped Kalakak's people find a suitable site for their new village. Fortunately, it was spring in the southern hemisphere, ideal for planting. Although they knew the people would have to handle the agriculture on their own eventually, the spiderbots were programmed to help with plowing and harrowing so crops could be planted almost immediately.

Then Parn, Ana, and Mehany taught Kalakak's people to identify star pepper trees. They taught them to hack down the trees and tear out the roots that linked the trees together into a destructive network. The people liked how well and brightly the stage one trees burned, but the spindling stage two trees were too explosive and were saved for special religious occasions.

Casualties from the crossing were few. Just two died from stress and from crowding. Thousands were saved. A quick genetic sample determined enough diversity for the population to safely grow and spread indefinitely. With such a successful operation, it was no wonder that the people concluded Ana was a manifestation of the godhead. She had to accept prayers and offerings everywhere she went. She graciously accepted them and in exchange she gave medications and nutritional supplements. Mamillo found it easy to adapt the immune converters to Kalakak's people. They were similar to several species already in the database, and the new ecosystem was well within the normal parameters for human habitation. Sicknesses were few, but enough for Mamillo to demonstrate the effectiveness of his healing. This improved Ana's status even further and Mamillo was, to his embarrassment, named a demigod.

Mehany and Parn had to settle for being angels. They were known to be good, and powerful, but they were believed to serve Ana's will. Saicy relished her role as adversary or "devil." She liked the fear she inspired when she walked through the village. Once she learned what the people's folklore said about the devil, she even dressed the part.

After a few tendays, everything seemed to be going well enough that Saicy announced her intention to return to Xythas. Based on market prices when they left, the partial star pepper cargo and the information of the new seeds' trajectory amounted to a small fortune for Parn. Saicy said she expected their story to yield even more profits. Mehany was also eager to return, but, for his part, Parn wasn't.

He had started using his carving skills to shape trees into portraits. He had done Kalakak and Saicy. They looked good, but he knew he could do better. He looked forward to having more time and quiet to improve his carving.

Then one night, Ana surprised him by saying, "We should have a child here."

"What?" Parn asked. They were walking a path that led away from the village and the ship, down the slope to the side of a lake. Ana took several steps in silence before answering.

"I love you. I know you love me. I want to have a child with you, but I don't like the thought of having one back on Xythas. To bring a child up in that caste system of wealth, bordered by walls and finances, it just makes me sad. But here, it seems a child could be whatever they wanted."

They reached the edge of the water. It shone with moonlight, but also the smooth surface reflected the planet in the sky that had turned bright red. Parn reached down and freed a round stone from the sandy bank. He looked back up the slope at the bright bonfire of the village. Then he looked back down at the smooth surface of the lake. He threw the stone out. It splashed quietly, and the ripples distorted the view of the reflected lights.

He smiled. "Yeah. I think you're right. Mamillo can leave us equipment and medications that can protect us. And the baby. And then I won't have to go back to the money and fight the claims. Saicy and her lawyers can handle that."

Ana hugged him. "We'll take some extra rations from the ship, too. And we'll have the mecha for protection if we need it."

Parn cocked his head. "You talked to Saicy about this already?"

"Of course. She said it was fine as long as I got footage. She thinks it could really help with the survivalist market."

"Can't argue with that."

Ana bent down and pulled her own stone from the sand. She threw it into the lake with a soft plunk. The ripples from Parn's stone hadn't completely vanished, but they were absorbed seamlessly into the ripples from Ana's stone. "Then we're decided," she said, and clung to Parn. He clung to her, too. Not for life, nor hope, nor profit. Just love. And that seemed to be enough.

Now That You've Finished

If you enjoyed *Star Pepper*, let me know. Write a review on Amazon, Goodreads, and wherever else you look for inspiration about what to read.

Check WWW.WriterMC.com to check out my previous titles. You can also sign up for my newsletter to get updates from me, other writers I know, and artists I support.

Thank you for reading.